Sophy

Rescued Widows, Spinsters, and Brides

Book 1

Elaine Manders

Copyright ©2022, Elaine Manders

All Rights Reserved

This is a work of fiction. Names, characters, and incidents are products of the author's imagination, and are not to be construed as real. Any resemblance to actual events or persons, other than known historical figures, is purely coincidental. Situations, places, and dates may have been moved around to fit the story. Except for review quotes, this book may not be reproduced, in whole or in part, without the written consent of the author.

Scripture references are taken from the King James Version (KJV) of the Bible.

Cover Design: Virginia McKevitt

May every reader be blessed and the Lord be magnified.

Chapter 1

Dakota Territory, 1884

The riverboat horn blasted, jolting Caleb Beckham so badly he hit his head on the timber ceiling of the Red Princess's hull.

Martin Schneider's booming laugh followed the third horn blast as he slapped Caleb on the back. "You never get used to that, my friend."

"Never. I'm glad we're getting off at this stop." Caleb hefted his saddlebags, his only luggage, over his shoulders. "It'll take me a few minutes to get Ginger. We can meet on the dock."

"It will take me a little while to gather my things. I think it would be best to find that fellow with the oxen before I claim my wagon at the mercantile. Clingenhoff, I think his name was. Or maybe Clingerhoff." Martin chuckled. "Ah, we'll find him, my friend."

"That's a good idea. I'd appreciate it if you'd go with me to talk to the man. You know more about oxen than I do. I don't want to buy a yoke of untrained beasts."

"Clingerhoff is an honest man, I believe, but I'll go with you. Maybe we'll find a restaurant along the way."

"Can I help you carry your stuff?" Martin had bought a good many items from the riverboat stops on their journey from the Canadian border. The men had met at a lumber mill where they'd both put in orders for lumber milled from the great Canadian forests.

Caleb had wanted to buy enough lumber to build a house, but the prices changed his mind. Besides he hadn't found a good homesite yet. It was a blessing he'd met Martin, who'd been farming his land claim for almost five years and shared a world of information—things Caleb hadn't even thought of.

Martin waved him on. "No, I can manage here. You go on and get our horses. I'll wait here. It'll take a while for the crew to clear the boat."

The stables weren't far, but it was busy with other travelers like him who'd left their horses here before boarding the Red Princess. Since it would take Martin awhile to join him, he could afford to wait.

Caleb had struck up an instant friendship with the burly German. When Martin confirmed

Sophy

he had been homesteading for over four years, Caleb knew this man could answer his questions, and he wasn't wrong.

Martin named the steps Caleb would have to take to claim his land, turn it into a working farm, and prove it within five years. His new friend listed the material needed to get started and offered to introduce Caleb to a man who had trained oxen for sell.

That last part was important. Caleb had already figured out most of the rest, but he'd need a yoke of oxen to work the land, now covered with thick waist-high prairie grass. He wasn't surprised when Martin warned it would take two years to put in crops since the grass had to be plowed and turned, then plowed again the second year.

Martin was excited to announce that he'd made a profit this year and still had some winter wheat to send to market. True, he and his family still lived in a soddy, but he had plans to build a real house next year. His Sophy deserved that much.

It was plain Martin loved his wife. His conversation was filled with Sophy this and Sophy that. He was anxious to get back, since he'd left Sophy alone with their two children—a girl and a boy. Martin was proud of his Sophy.

Caleb enjoyed Martin's talk about his farm—his family, but it made him lonely. His time trekking along the prairie had him lonelier than he'd ever been, and that was even when he'd caught the riverboat at the end of each day. What would it be like living out there by himself?

It isn't good for man to be alone.

That verse had never hit him as hard as during this trip. And all the talk about Martin's wife had him thinking maybe he should get married before staking his claim. Now, he was beginning to understand that working the soil, building a home, demanded a helpmate.

He just couldn't picture Clarise in this wild land. When he'd first mentioned homesteading in North Dakota, the idea excited her. It would be a great adventure, she'd said. But she didn't know the difficulties—the back-breaking work, the desolation—awaiting her out here where nothing but nature lived. Clarise was such a friendly, garrulous woman. How would she manage on this land where the near neighbor could be a two-day wagon ride away?

If nothing else, this trip had convinced Caleb it would be better for him to claim his land first and build a house. How could he bring a wife into the wilderness without even a dwelling to cover her head?

Martin had laid out answers to that question. A man could claim one hundred and sixty acres if he were married, but just eighty as a single man. Yet did he really want that much land without anyone to help him work it? Besides, he really wanted to breed horses and only farm a few acres. After talking to Martin, he'd decided he should raise mules, too. Mules were hard to come by, according to Martin and they sold for higher prices than horses out on the plains.

Caleb had been scouting the Dakota Territory from the Canadian border, seeking the best land for a claim. He wanted a plot close to the Red River, but already most of the best sites, especially in the south, had been claimed. He'd decided to come back to Twin Forks, buy supplies, a wagon and oxen team, then return to file his claim on the best site he'd found, though it was a mile from the river.

His new friend had looked over Caleb's proposed claim and suggested he find another. Martin's farm was in a prime location and he said the section just west was available. Just talking to Martin, Caleb could tell the man wanted a neighbor he could get along with. Apparently, he'd had one who'd been lazy and let his place run down before leaving the area.

There was a better chance Clarise would become acclimated to the land if she had a neighbor lady, and Caleb knew Martin's Sophy would become a good friend.

The way Martin described the location and the condition of the land, Caleb was excited to return with the farmer. It was an answer to prayer, and he had prayed every mile of the way along the Red River.

The stables were bustling, and it took a few minutes to catch the attention of a stable boy to bring out Ginger. As he waited for Martin's horse, he turned and scanned the crowd of men, hoping to sight the tall, dark-haired man.

In one blinding flash, an explosion blasted the air, almost knocking him down. He circled around to see what had happened. It wasn't hard to tell. Flames as high as the tree tops rose above the boat.

Martin. Caleb found himself caught up in the mass of shouting, cursing men, some running from the river, some, like him, running to it. "Martin! Martin!" he shouted, but his voice blew away on the hot wind.

Men crowded the dock, some still on the boat, trying to get the cargo off, saving what they could. Surely, Martin wasn't still in the hull. Caleb had to be sure.

Flames licked the stern as he ran up the gangplank. The captain stood at the bottom, directing the boatmen. He was too occupied to even see Caleb's frantic hand-waving. Men weaved around the scattered storage bins, headed for the hatch, blocking Caleb. Only with a great deal of pushing and shoving, did he manage to get on the boat.

Smoke billowed over him, making it impossible to see in the dark hole. "Martin!" He couldn't find the stairs, so he dropped into the hull. Then he saw devilish red streaks licking the planks. The whole thing would soon be filled with flames.

Sophy

Maybe if he crawled on the bottom where the smoke was thinner.

Sure enough, there was Martin lying prone on the floor. Impossible to tell whether he was unconscious or dead, even though the light was better down here. One glance to the walls showed Caleb why. There at where the water line would be on the boat's sides, the boards glowed red. This thing was going to sink within minutes. Maybe seconds. Water was already sloshing over his feet.

But without help, how was he to get the man out of this hole? Still on all fours, Caleb looked around wildly. *God, help me find a way.*

There on the right side, a timber—from where he didn't know—had fallen at a slope and rested a couple of feet on the still intact deck. Caleb's only choice was to drag Martin to the top on that six-inch wide plank.

With no time left to rethink his strategy, he got a hold of the big, unconscious man and dragged him to the sloping plank. *Lord, give me strength.* Caleb knew for sure he wouldn't have enough strength to get Martin out. The smoke burned his eyes and, despite the bandana around his mouth and nose, he could hardly breathe.

Blood rushed in his ears as his heart pounded against his ribs. His eyes burned, making it impossible to keep his lids fully open. Where was the strength coming from? Where, Lord? But he had no choice. Both Martin and he would die if they didn't get out of this inferno.

With not enough air to shout for help, and the boat taking on water, Caleb dragged Martin to the plank. Inch by painful inch, he took one backward step at a time. Somehow, he kept ahead of the water, though dizzy and his lungs bursting for want of air.

Miraculously, he reached the deck. The captain dropped what he was doing and took one side of Martin. Caleb and the captain had just cleared the gangplank when the boat sank fast, and within moments was completely submerged. The only evidence left that a boat had sat there on the slow-moving river was bubbles rising to the top of the water.

They dragged Martin onto a clear space on the grass. "I'll send the doctor," the captain said, then left Caleb alone with his friend. He examined the man and in the clear light of day he realized Martin was burned much worse than he'd thought. Most of his shirt was burned off him and his chest was covered in soot and charred skin. His face, too, was black.

Caleb dropped to his knees and hovered over Martin's face. Under the soot, blood seeped through cracks. There was nothing to tell him the man was still alive except the rise and fall of his chest.

"Martin, can you hear me?"

Martin's blackened lips moved, but no words came. Instead, the wounded man lifted his arm and pointed to his stomach. No, he was pointing to his money belt. He'd not taken it off at any point during his trip, he'd told Caleb. It held the money to buy supplies along with a list Sophy had given him.

Caleb looked up to the different groups of men and found where the other injured had been lain. A man, probably the doctor, walked among them. He cupped his hand to his mouth and shouted. "Get a doctor over here fast."

Truthfully, he feared Martin was beyond a doctor's help. He lifted prayers to the only One Who could help. Within moments, his prayers were interrupted when the doctor bent over Martin.

He found the doctor's sorrowful gaze. "I'm sorry. He's not going to make it. There's nothing we can do." The doctor left, and Caleb noticed Martin still trying to speak, his finger still pointing to his money belt.

A sound like a wheeze broke through, and Caleb leaned over, straining to hear. "Heeep...Heeeelp Sophy." A puff of smoke escaped as Martin spoke, confirming the doctor's pronouncement.

Helpless, Caleb watched the puffs as the man tried to breathe, then his eyes fluttered and his hand fell, his chest stilled. Caleb pushed back on his heels and lifted his face to the sky. "Lord God, take Your servant, Martin, into Your kingdom. And thank You, Lord, for giving me the chance to know him."

He worked with Martin's belt buckle but it wouldn't budge. The metal might have fused in the fire. How hot must that first blast have been? He slipped the knife out of his boot and sliced through the leather to release the money belt. He would take only enough money to provide Martin with a decent funeral and count the rest so he could give it all to his wife, Sophy.

A shame she couldn't be here for her husband's funeral. A shame he couldn't take Martin's body home so he could be buried on his own land. But the weather was still hot and too much time needed to buy the supplies, wagon, and oxen before he could make the journey back to Martin's homestead. And the trip itself would take a week or more with a lumbering wagon pulled by oxen. If he made good time.

He thought of the woman, out there on the prairie, who'd already spent he didn't know how many days alone with two young children. And each day she'd be looking south, waiting for a husband who would never return.

Caleb would claim the land beside Mrs. Schneider's farm. He wished he could buy her place, buildings, stock, and all, but he didn't have enough money to do that. He had no doubt the woman would have to sell to somebody, though. She couldn't possibly hang onto it, even if she could find someone to work the land.

Mrs. Schneider wouldn't be able to trust anyone except her family to help her. Surely she did have some family left, though Martin hadn't

Sophy

mentioned any, nor where they'd come from. It was a shame.

Caleb would buy up his provisions and leave her money intact. She'd need it when she returned to her family. Because that was the only thing she could do.

After speaking to the undertaker and making arrangements for Martin's funeral, Caleb stopped by the post office to send his letter home. Before the accident he'd almost decided to drop his plans to claim a homesite this year and go home to his parents' southern Illinois farm. He needed to have a serious talk with Clarise. She might want to call off their wedding when she realized how desolate and dangerous the Dakota prairie was.

Homesickness weighed on his shoulders like a heavy blanket. How wonderful it would be to sit around his parents' table. Hear his father's advice. His brother's teasing. His mother's sweet voice. The meal he ate at a small café only increased his yearning for Mama's good cooking.

But even if he didn't have to deliver supplies back to his future homestead and help the young widow pack up and leave, it was best he not run home. Because his parents' place was no longer his home. His older brother and sister-in-law would take over the Illinois farm. He could offer Clarise nothing but a soddy in a field of waist-high prairie grass.

Caleb had decided to leave Illinois long ago

and forge his own way. Make a life for himself in the Dakota Territory, and with God's help, he'd do it.

He'd asked around town for Mr. Clingerhoff, the man with oxen, but no one knew him, nor did they know anyone who had oxen for sale. Caleb made another decision without his father's advice. The stables owner had a three-year-old stallion for sale. Caleb could tell the horse was superior stock, a huge quarter horse, a stud for his Percheron mare. Together, they'd produce the work horses that were in such high demand out here. He'd have to farm his land, too, of course, and grow corn and oats, but the horses would be the means of a good living. Maybe Clarise would wait a few years until he would build a decent house. One fitting for a bride.

It was a gamble. Most settlers considered the prairie good for nothing but wheat and corn, acres and acres of it, but they couldn't grow those crops without good stock. The way he saw it, everything and every direction one took was a gamble.

Grand Forks had disappointed Caleb at first sight. With a name like that he'd expected more than a few buildings strewn at the junction of the Red River and Red Lake River, but the town had everything a settler would want. It was still little more than it had started out—a trading post for the natives and French fur traders. But that was all right. It would grow as more people arrived.

Sophy

He used Martin's list to buy supplies at the mercantile and feed stores on the chance Sophy did want to stay on her farm. He thought of her as Sophy instead of Mrs. Schneider or Martin's wife. Maybe because Martin had used her name over and over again, like a drum beat he wanted everyone to hear.

The room at the boardinghouse wasn't much, but it would be the last decent cover he'd have for the week it would take him to reach the Schneider farm. The next morning he called on Smithers, the man who had a covered wagon for sale and hoped it was still for sale. It would be his housing until he could build a soddy.

The wagon was still available, though it had a rip in the canvas and a wheel Caleb feared wouldn't make it for the trip. Smithers just happened to have a spare wagon wheel for a price. Shaking his head, Caleb paid the man and harnessed his horses to the rig. He wouldn't bother looking for oxen. These strong horses could plow his fields. Maybe.

Now all he had to do was stop by the mercantile to pick up the supplies.

As he drove the team past the river, a man carrying a gunny sack, making his way to the river's edge, snagged Caleb's attention. He halted the horses. There was something strange about the sack. Looked like it was moving. That sack held a cat or dog unless he missed his guess. Something Caleb wouldn't abide was cruelty to animals.

He urged the team in front of the man and pulled the brake. "Howdy." He greeted the man with a smile to show he meant no harm.

"Howdy," the man said. "Can I help you?"

"You might can. I'm Caleb Beckham. I was just passing through and wondered what's in your sack?"

"Joe Lemmon." Lemmon set the sack on the ground and the men shook hands. In answer to Caleb's question, Lemmon pulled out a shaggy puppy. "From a litter of eight. Couldn't give her away. Most folks don't want females." He laughed. "Suppose you know why."

The pup squirmed and whined as Lemmon held her up by the scruff. "I might want her if you're giving her away." Caleb said.

Lemmon held the wiggling pup up between them. "Hear that, Sunny. Looks like you get a reprieve. Now I don't have to lie to the young'uns."

Caleb took the puppy and examined her. She had good markings with ears, back and tail the color of a golden retriever, the head, lower body and legs almost white. "She looks to be about three months old and has some sheepdog in her." He glanced at the man. "You already named her, huh?"

"Well the young'uns did. She's real good with young'uns, and might be a decent herding dog with some training."

Sophy

"I'm counting on that." Caleb scratched the dog behind her ears and she licked his hand. He was hoping Sunny was good with children because Martin's two little ones would need a distraction when they understood their father wouldn't be coming back.

He thanked Mr. Lemmon and found a piece of rope to tie around Sunny's neck. He settled her on the wagon seat and pulled a piece of jerky out of his pocket. Why hadn't he thought of getting a dog before? Sunny would fill in those empty, lonely hours as he worked on his settlement.

As he left Grand Forks, his thoughts wandered back to Sophy and how he would tell her her future had changed in the single moment of a riverboat explosion.

Chapter 2

Out here on the prairie, nothing went to waste, least of all an animal skin. If not for that, Sophy Schneider would have thrown the deer hide she had laid out on the backyard table as far as she could toss it. The slime of deer brains and ashes had finally loosened the hair, and now she had little time to scrape the skin clean.

Not even a breeze blew across the prairie this morning to carry off the stench filling her nostrils, threatening to cast up her accounts. She slung the mess off her scraper and held it suspended a moment, her glance traveling to where Heidi and Marty played near her kitchen garden. Heidi was almost four and had to be watched at all times. If she strayed off into the tall grass, she might never be found. Sophy had heard horror stories.

Marty, their nickname for Martin, Jr., could crawl now, and he'd follow Heidi everywhere.

Sophy

She worked the kinks out of her shoulders and pulled another section of hide across the boards, closing her eyes against the foul smell. The quiet was disconcerting. Usually the wind hummed as it blew low over the grass, giving one the impression that the grass moved in waves like the sea.

That was why the wagons carrying new settlers west were called prairie schooners. Sophy had become used to the sound and when it was missing, she noticed it and yearned for its return, as if it were an old friend. She wasn't as fond of the wind in winter, but even when it shrieked around the eaves of their soddy, she wasn't frightened. She knew the thick walls would stand. She was even getting used to the howling winter wind.

She heard the children's voices and knew they were fine, but glanced up to make sure. Heidi was showing Marty a worm she'd found in the garden. "Heidi, don't let him eat that thing."

"I won't, Ma."

Satisfied the children were all right, Sophy peered across the southern prairie. Nothing appeared in the endless grass all the way to the horizon. Even after four years she'd not become oriented to the vastness of the prairie. She knew it would take someone driving a wagon a half day to disappear below the horizon, seemingly moving slowly, growing smaller until they were only dots where the sky met earth.

She knew this in her mind, but still couldn't

accept it. Even when Martin appeared, it would take hours to reach the farm. Everything was like that out here. Everything took time.

The Lord had taught Sophy patience that first year when she, pregnant with Heidi, and Martin lived in the covered wagon. She cooked in the firepit. Baked in a Dutch oven. Fried corn cakes with goose grease in a spider. That was before Martin had the well dug. So most of the meal preparation time had involved hauling water from the muddy river, straining it twice. After the meal, she'd have to wash the dishes in the river, which was half a mile from their homesite. And washing clothes—that was a back-breaking job lasting from dawn till dark.

She finished the section of hide and stood to stretch, releasing a deep sigh. She'd soon be through with this part of the tanning process. The hide would dry hard and then she'd moisten it and pull it over the edge of the contraption Martin had made for that purpose. It, too, was back-breaking work and she never got the leather as supple as she'd like. Martin said he'd ask the man who owned the leather goods store in Grand Forks if he knew the best way to tan leather.

Was that what was taking him so long? He should have returned two days ago. She wasn't worried yet. He'd have to depend on the riverboat schedule. The captain would drop him off about two miles south of the homestead and he'd load the supplies in their wagon which he'd left with Mr. Rand, the old man who lived on the river and traded with the riverboat travelers.

She returned her attention to the deer skin. The squaws chewed the hide to soften it, but that set her stomach roiling. She might have to work it longer this way, but so be it. The leather would make her a new pair of gloves and Martin a vest.

The next time she looked up she thought she saw a dot on the horizon. Could it be Martin? She crossed her arms and clasped her hands around her elbows, staring at the spot that grew larger ever so slowly.

The small object was white which meant it was a covered wagon. Certainly not Martin, since they'd taken the canvas off their wagon when they moved into the soddy. Another sodbuster come to claim a section of land. She was used to them since they drove by every few days. Most stopped, full of questions about life on the prairie. Usually a man came with his family, sometimes just a wife. Occasionally, a single man drove the wagon, intending to build a soddy before his family joined him.

Anyone driving a covered wagon probably held no evil intent. This wasn't the wild west like she'd read about, but since she was alone, she wouldn't take a chance. She left the hide and collected the children.

"Ma, I'm hungry," Heidi said as soon as they got inside.

Marty started to cry. "Tookie...tookie."

"Fine, it's near lunchtime." She tied Marty to his highchair and ordered Heidi. "Go wash up and bring a washcloth to wipe off your brother's face and hands."

She'd heat up the stew and biscuits for her and the children, but she had something else to do first. With a grunt, she lifted the rifle off its rack held in place by pegs driven into the soddy wall. After placing it on the table by the dry sink, she turned her attention to the stove.

Marty was still crying and pounding on the table. "Heidi, don't dawdle," she called to her daughter. She carried warm water from the reservoir to the sink and washed her hands with lye soap. There was nothing else that would get off the nasty residue left on her hands after tanning a hide.

She dished up the stew and set their plates on the table. Marty was able to feed himself with his hands, so she fished the potato and carrot chunks out of the stew so he could handle them. Then sat down to her own bowl.

"You forgot the milk, Ma," Heidi complained.

Nerves fluttered in Sophy's chest. It was hard paying attention to her children with strangers coming. Oh, how she wished Martin was here. She shot up and fetched the milk from the icebox.

She filled Heidi's cup and the canning jar used as a bottle for Marty. She'd weened Marty

Sophy

early to give her more time with the chores, and he'd become quite proficient with the bottle. Of course, she'd ordered half a dozen rubber nipples to make milk bottles for the baby. One of these was held around the rim of the jar with a piece of twine.

Here on the prairie one had to improvise often, schedule meals like your life depended on it, and plan for unexpected hardships like grasshopper invasions, hail storms, or drought.

Nothing was ever wasted. Rain barrels caught runoff from the roof. Wash water was saved to water the garden. Every scrap of paper was saved to write notes or letters. Every bit of fabric was reused, from old clothes to quilt blocks. Very little leftover food made its way to the slop jar. Chicken, beef and pig bones were kept to cook for stock used in soups and stews.

"Heidi, you and Marty stay here at the table until I come back." Sophy hefted the rifle and went outside to see how far the stranger had traveled. Her heart flipped when she realized he was minutes away. She'd assumed oxen pulled the wagon, but instead, the rigging of two fine horses jingled as they pranced across the prairie, left the tall grass pressed down into a straight ribbon behind, all the way to the horizon.

A horse tagged behind the wagon. She squinted to get a better look. If she didn't know better, she'd think that was Sukie, Martin's roan mare.

The traveler turned toward the house, assuring her he meant to stop here. That didn't mean he intended harm, she told herself. He might have followed her smoke from afar and hoped he'd find a home-cooked meal. He looked too young to have a family—but maybe a wife was hidden in the back of the wagon.

Sophy didn't have time to check the rifle, but she knew Martin had cleaned, oiled, and loaded it before he left. He knew she was adept at shooting because he'd taught her that first season. She'd turned into a good hunter, but shooting an animal was different from shooting a man. She didn't know if she had the nerve to shoot another human being.

Her pulse raced as it always did when a stranger approached, but she kept the rifle down for now.

Chapter 3

Caleb had imagined every possible way he'd greet Martin's widow, but never in all of the different scenarios that filtered through his brain had he imagined the lady would greet him with a gun. He pulled in the reins of Sibbie, his mare, and the new stallion, as yet unnamed, a good ten yards from Mrs. Schneider, then approached her with hands raised.

"Mrs. Schneider? Howdy, I'm Caleb Beckham. Ma'am, your husband and I got to be friends on the riverboat."

She lowered her rifle below her waist. "Where is Martin? He should have returned home by now."

Caleb coughed as he took off his hat and dared to lower his hands. "Ma'am, that's why I'm here. There was an accident." He took in the perimeter of the house. It was typical of a soddy, maybe a little larger than most. Two front windows were more than most soddies would have. There was no porch, but two long benches formed an L to the left of the door.

"Could we sit down so I can tell you about it?" He didn't need to sit, but she did. She'd turned pale at the mention of an accident. He watched her face blanch, her lips tremble.

"All right." She turned and went to sit at the end of one of the benches. He took it as an invitation to sit on the other bench.

He hunched over, his hat between his knees and released a long sigh. He was about to destroy this woman's future dreams of building a life out here. When he looked out at the waving fields of wheat almost ready to harvest, he knew she wouldn't be able to remain and do all the work such an operation would demand.

"I'm listening," she urged.

He didn't know any other way to say it. "I'm powerful sorry, ma'am. Your husband, Martin, was killed in a riverboat explosion."

She just stared at him for a minute like she waited for him to tell her he was mistaken. Then she bound from the bench and sprang back, her gun poised. "I don't believe you. I'd've heard about something like that."

"It's the truth, ma'am. Martin and I became friends because we both slept in the boat's hold, right near the boilers. He didn't suffer. You can comfort yourself with that." That wasn't exactly true, but Martin didn't live long enough to suffer

Sophy

much. "He told me to bring you your supplies." He reached into his coat and pulled out Martin's money belt. "I used my own money for the supplies. Here's his. I figured you'd need it."

She just stared at him, her hands holding the gun shook, making him nervous. "He asked me to help you and the children. I'm going to claim the section that was abandoned, so I can use the supplies if you want to go back to family."

"I don't have any family," she said. "Even if I did, I'm not going anywhere. Martin and I have worked too hard on this farm. We're one year away from proving it up."

Caleb coughed into his fist. Out of the side of his eye he could see the acres heavy with wheat. "You can't harvest all that," he nodded toward the fields, "by yourself."

"Martin contracted with a threshing company. I'll do what I must."

Her beautiful face was so pale, and the gun shook like it would fall from her hands. She was probably in shock. They stood staring into each other's eyes. Finally, she leaned the rifle by the side of the house.

"Ma...ma...Marty wants down." A child's voice pulled Sophy's gaze from Caleb.

She opened the door and glanced back at him. "If you'd come in, please."

He heard Sunny, still tied to the wagon,

barking, but Sunny would have to wait. He followed Sophy.

Caleb gave the room a sweeping glance, hardly believing how nice the inside was. Though outside the house looked like any other soddy—maybe bigger—the inside might have been any wooden farmhouse. The narrow plank floor gleamed, while wider boards, painted white, covered the walls. A leather upholstered sofa and chair accompanying a rocking chair anchored a pleasant seating area. White chintz curtains hung at the windows. A wall partially hid the kitchen, but an oak table and chairs took up the right side of the room.

A baby sat in one of the dining chairs and when he saw his mother he started crying—screaming was a better way to describe it. "Marty wants down," the little girl repeated.

Sophy wobbled as her hand flew to her head. Caleb swooped in to catch her just before she hit the floor. He took the swooning woman to the sofa and laid her down.

"Who are you?" Heidi asked in a voice Caleb could barely hear above her brother's shrieking.

He looked around wildly as if searching for someone to help. "I'm Caleb." In wide strides he reached the baby and untied the rag that held him. Marty—wasn't that the name Martin had mentioned—stopped his screaming and stared at Caleb with large blue eyes.

Not knowing what to do with the child and

Sophy

needing to attend Sophy, he set Marty on the floor and addressed Heidi. "Can you take care of your brother while I wake up your ma?"

"I'll go to our room and he'll follow me," Heidi said. "He follows me everywhere." Sure enough, as she skipped through the opening that must have led to the bedroom, Marty crawled after her.

Caleb spied a dishrag and dipped it into the stove's reservoir. The water was hot, but he cooled it by waving it in the air as he hastened to Sophy, glad to find some color returning to her cheeks.

As soon as he wiped her face with the cold rag, her eyes popped open. He could see the different emotions in their blue depths. Shock. Disbelief. Realization. Sorrow. "The children?"

She made to rise and he helped her to her still shaky feet. He kept his hand on her shoulder for support. "They went to their room." He smiled. "Why don't you sit over there at the table and let me get you a cup of coffee." He'd noticed the coffeepot on the stove. Since it was still morning, he expected it was still hot.

A slight nod indicated her agreement. Caleb kept his arm around her shoulders and held her right hand as he helped her to the kitchen table. She was so small, the top of head barely reaching to his shoulder. But he could feel her strength, even as she walked stiffly beside him. Her calloused hands told him this was a woman who did hard work. Still, even as strong as she was, no matter how used she was to hard work, she couldn't keep up this large farm and take care of two young children alone.

When she came to her senses, she'd realize that.

"The cups are in that cupboard. Get yourself a cup, too." Sophy pointed to a pretty white cabinet detailed with blue flowers. His ma had a similar one. A Hoover cabinet, it was called, with bins for flour and sugar. The flour bin had an attached sifter. Cannisters lined the back of the counter. Sophy had a nice kitchen, far better than he would have expected in this unsettled land. The iron stove had six lids, a big oven, a compartment to keep food warm, and a large reservoir. Martin must have done very well, indeed.

But for all Caleb knew, Sophy had brought money to the marriage. No wonder she didn't want to leave, but he didn't see how she could stay.

He snagged the coffee pot on the way back to the table. Sophy was staring into space as he poured her cup full. "Do you take cream or sugar?"

Long moments passed before she looked at him like she'd just noticed he was there. "I used all the cream in the children's oatmeal this morning. The sugar is over by the sink. There are clean spoons on the rack."

He poured his cup, then brought the sugar

Sophy

over and took the chair opposite Sophy. Since she'd started drinking her coffee black, he assumed she didn't want the sugar. Taking a chair opposite her, he sat and gripped the cup with both hands. "I took it upon myself to contact the Lutheran Church in Grand Rapids and the pastor there gave him a proper burial. Martin told me he was a Lutheran."

The hint of a smile played on her lips. "Martin was a great believer. He lived and breathed his faith."

"I can attest to that," Caleb said. "I hadn't known him for a few hours before I knew he was a good Christian man. I'm certain he's in that mansion the Lord prepared for him."

Her throat moved in a swallow. "I know that for a fact," she croaked.

The patter of little bare feet slapped the floor behind them. "Ma, Marty is stinky."

Sophy started to get up, but he held out his palm. "Go ahead and finish your coffee. I'll change him."

"Do you have children, Mr. Beckham?" Her voice still sounded strained, and his heart ached for her.

"No ma'am, I'm not married, but I have two nephews." He got up. "Heidi can show me where the diapers are."

He saw the shine of tears in her eyes and she worked her mouth as if trying her best to hold them back. "Ma'am, why don't you go ahead and cry. It'll do you good."

She sobbed, a look of sheer pain etching her face as she tipped her head toward the child. "I'll have to tell her."

Heidi had to be told her father wasn't coming back. But did a three-year-old understand death? "It'll be hard. If it was me, I'd just tell her her pa went to Heaven." He didn't know if Sophy shared her husband's belief, but he was confident she did and believed Martin had truly gone to Heaven. "Maybe tell her God wanted her pa now and he didn't have a choice." The little girl must be assured her pa didn't abandon her.

Sophy nodded, her lips pressed tightly together, tears streaming down her cheeks.

"After I change Marty, I'll take him outside to meet my dog. That way, you'll have Heidi to yourself. She needs to know why you're sad." He took a few steps backward and added, "She needs to know it's all right for her to be sad."

Why was he giving Sophy this advice? She surely knew her daughter better than he did. It was just the woman looked so forlorn and overwhelmed. And he'd promised Martin he'd help his family.

He turned from her and made his way toward Marty's cries. After he'd diapered the boy, he crossed the cheerful parlor, tickling Marty under the chin to distract him from his

Sophy

mother's and sister's voices.

Marty had obviously never seen a dog, so Caleb set him beyond the barking Sunny's reach until he'd lengthened the rope to give her room to run around. Curiosity overcame fear and within a couple of minutes dog and boy were playing together.

Caleb let his gaze rove around the farm, from the fields to the barn and corral. All of the outbuildings were stick-built, but it wasn't unusual for farmers to build better barns than their houses.

Martin had built onto the soddy. Whitewashed siding surfaced the back of the structure, and a roof of cedar shakes covered the whole house. Martin probably made the shakes with his own hands from the trees growing along the river. Then Caleb remembered Martin had ordered lumber to build a new house. What would Sophy do when the wood arrived?

He tilted his head back and stared at the sky, looking for answers that so far had evaded him. *Lord, what is this widow and her children going to do? There isn't a congregation of Your people here to help them as Your word commands.*

Most of the time he had to wait for answers to his prayers. This time he didn't have to wait.

He knew what he had to do.

Chapter 4

Heidi's wails tore at Sophy's heart, but she couldn't stop her own sobs. The child finally grew quiet, her face buried on Sophy's breast, and her tear-stained face lifted. "Who's going to take care of us without Pa?" Sophy had no answer.

"I want my pa to come back from Heaven." Heidi whispered after crying on Sophy's shoulder until hers and her mothers' tears were finally spent.

Sophy rested her chin on the child's head. "I'll take care of you and Marty. Don't you worry about that. We'll be fine."

Heidi was a smart little girl. "But you take care of us in the house and garden. Pa takes care of the horses and cows and works out in the fields."

Sophy stiffened her spine. This was Caleb's opinion. She'd seen it in his eyes when she told

Sophy

him they'd be staying here on the homestead. She brushed back the fine hair on Heidi's forehead and pressed a kiss to her temple. "We'll make do. You and Marty will grow and be able to do more."

Disbelief furrowed Heidi's brow. "What about Cabub? He could take care of the horses and cows and pigs and—"

Sophy cut her off. "That's a thought. Mr. Beckham is going to claim the homestead where the Muntz couple lived. You remember the lady and man who lived in their wagon? If Mr. Beckham does take that land, he could build his house there, and we'll be neighbors. I expect he'd be willing to help us." She bit her lip, the idea just forming in her mind. There was money enough to hire him to take care of the stock...work the fields.

Her chest bloomed with hope. She slipped Heidi off her lap. Why hadn't she thought of that as soon as Caleb had mentioned it? Maybe that's what he was suggesting when he said he'd promised Martin he'd help the family.

Of course, it must be. Martin had always hired a hand or two during harvest. He'd probably promised Caleb a job on the farm. That's why he'd looked at her like she'd grown a third eye. She even managed a smile as she got to her feet.

A dog barked, snagging Heidi's attention. She tore away from her mother and dashed to the front door. Sophy followed because the door was too heavy for Heidi to open—and she, too, was curious.

Heidi scampered ahead of her out the door, down the steps, sprinting straight to the puppy. Marty sat on the grass, laughing while the dog ran around and around the baby, then scudding to a stop and licking Marty's face, making him giggle harder.

When Heidi joined the circle beside her brother, the dog stopped and jumped right in her face, toppling her backward and licking her face. It was as if her little girl had forgotten what she'd just heard about her father. She came up, laughing and lunging for the dog who teased her by bouncing just out of her reach.

Why hadn't they gotten a dog before now? They already had a bunch of barn cats. Heidi had tamed a couple of the cats, but she'd always wanted a dog. Sophy and Martin had talked about it. A dog would help with herding the cattle, if they ever got enough cattle to herd. A dog would be helpful watching the children. More importantly, a dog would alert them to danger.

Caleb's puppy was cute, and Sophy yearned to cuddle it herself. She walked up to where Caleb was unloading the supplies. "What's his name?"

He set the crate on the ground and wiped his brow with his shirtsleeve. "It's a girl, and her name is Sunny."

Sophy

Sophy couldn't resist kneeling to pet the puppy. "A good name, but she's small right now and not used to the wilds. We sometimes have wolves come out of the woods trying to carry off a chicken or pig. The horses and cows are kept in the barn so they are kept safe. I suggest you keep her in there, too."

"She'll sleep with me in the wagon until I get my soddy built."

Did he understand how long it might take one man to build a soddy? She rose to standing. "Well, you can stable your horses in our barn."

"Thank you, ma'am. You want me to put the food stuffs on the kitchen table?"

"That will be fine. There's nothing that will spoil. I'll put everything away later." She ran to the door to hold it open for him and followed him to the kitchen. They stored the food depending on what it was into the pantry or taken to the root cellar.

Martin had lined a corner of the back porch with shelves for canned goods, both home-made and bought. As Caleb reentered the kitchen from his last trip, Sophy held up the coffeepot. "Coffee's still warm. Want a cup? I fetched some cream from the cellar."

His smile gave her some confidence to ask if he'd hire on with the farm. She was asking a lot because he'd have to put his own plans on hold. After he'd taken his first sip, she said, "Martin was going to hire a live-in hand for the harvest. How would you like the job?"

He set his cup down and lifted one brow. "I intend to help you from here on out, ma'am—as a neighbor, not a hired hand. No need to hire anyone else except for the threshing crew you said was coming in." His smile would probably melt the heart of any woman except a new widow.

"Then we need to talk about the provisions. I counted the money you gave me. Nearly all of it's there. You must have bought them yourself." She seemed to remember he'd said that when he'd been telling her about Martin, but at that time all she could hear was her husband was gone.

He held his cup suspended. "That's right. I figured you'd want to leave and wouldn't need them. Since you're staying, you can pay me for half. I'll be living out of the wagon, so I won't need much, and I'll be hunting and fishing for fresh meat. I've heard the land is full of game."

He obviously didn't realize how cold Dakota's winters were. She let a few seconds slip by before adding, "I agree we'll have enough for all of us until you get your farm producing, but I'll pay for all of it. What you supply in fresh meat and fish will make up for what you use." She'd already stirred the cream in her coffee long enough to make butter, but he had to hear her out. "You can stay in the barn instead of your wagon. There's a small room in back where the hired hand stayed except on really cold nights.

Sophy

Then he'd lay his bedroll in front of the hearth. You can do the same."

She peered into his questioning grey eyes. "You'll have to do that," she said firmly. She wouldn't let a man freeze on her land.

He stared at the tablecloth, the one that took her a year to crochet. Martin had asked her why she put such a fancy cloth on their table where Heidi or Marty was bound to drop drink or food on it, maybe leaving stains that wouldn't come out. She'd replied that she wanted at least something fancy in their soddy, and if the children left stains, they would only be precious memories of when they were little.

Memories. She had plenty of her own happy childhood. When her mother and father were still alive. Then Pa had lost everything in the economic downturn. Maybe the soddy wasn't much, but it was so much better than that rat-infested apartment they'd lived in until the fire that took her parents. She'd been at school at the time.

How ironic that Martin had also died in a fire. Was everyone she loved doomed to die by fire?

The scrape of Caleb's chair startled her. "I appreciate the offer, ma'am, but it wouldn't be seemly for me to sleep in the same house with you and the children. The barn will be good enough."

Unseemly? Yes, back in New York it would

have been unseemly. "Will you do me a favor, Caleb? Stop calling me ma'am. We aren't in high society here. There isn't any other person for twenty miles, and if there is nobody to gossip, does it matter about what is seemly or not? Surely we can be on a first-name basis."

She heard a rumble of laughter before he answered. "I'd be pleased to call you Sophy if you call me Caleb—or Cabub, as Heidi does."

Her laughter surprised her. How could she laugh on the day she'd learned she'd lost her husband? "See, if we lived in society, I'd have to insist Heidi call you Mr. Cabub."

"Well, society or not, I think it's proper for neighbors to use first names, and we will be neighbors."

She didn't know what else to say, but found it hard to pull away from his sympathetic eyes.

As if he sensed their time was getting awkward, he got to his feet. "I'd better get back out there. Don't worry about the young'uns. I'll keep an eye on them."

"That's...kind of you, but I've been keeping an eye on them. I can see them through the window behind you."

He turned toward the window. "Those are nice windows. Most soddies don't have anything as nice."

She rose from the table, surprised to find her head still swimming. "I'd better start getting

Sophy

dinner ready. I expect you're hungry."

"Ma'am...Sophy...I'm not about to let you cook dinner. Let me get the rest of the supplies unloaded and the wagon broken down and I'll fry some ham for sandwiches."

The room had stopped spinning. "No, you have enough to do."

He reached out and took her forearm. "You're still in shock, Sophy. You need some time to heal and grieve. Why don't you come outside and sit on the bench? You can bring your sewing or just watch the children play. The air will do you good. And it won't be no trouble for me to fix our dinner.

"Back home when a family lost a loved one, the women of the church would bring in meals for the grieving family for a whole week." He released her arm and she clasped her hands in front. "Are you sure you don't want to go back to your relatives for a few weeks? I'd be glad to take you and keep up the place while you're gone."

"I don't have any relatives. Martin must not have told you. We met in an orphanage."

He drew in a breath. "I'm real sorry about that, Sophy. You need family at a time like this...or neighbors." He laid his hand on her back and eased her to the door. "Well, you have me. Not much, but between me and God, we'll see you through this hard time."

Caleb didn't know God had always held back His blessings from her except for Martin.

Elaine Manders

Now God had taken him. It wasn't worth getting her hopes up, looking for blessings. She'd been disappointed too many times. Back in the orphanage she had hopes that she'd take out each day and let those hopes parade across her mind to dull the pain of being abandoned. Then Martin had rescued her.

Now God had taken him. It was a refrain that kept ringing in her mind.

Caleb was right. The honeysuckle scented air carried on a soft breeze made her feel better. The children were already attached to the dog and to Caleb. Heidi followed him from one side of the wagon to the other, from the wagon to the barn, chattering away all the while. She'd be asking the hundreds of questions she'd peppered Martin with. The child's curiosity was astonishing. Sophy hadn't dared question her elders at all.

Apparently Heidi had momentarily forgotten her father wasn't coming home and had put Caleb in his place.

Not only that, but Marty followed Heidi. It was amusing really. They went from one place to the other in a little parade while Sunny, the dog, ran back and forth and around and around.

The dog must have some herding dog in her. Since Marty always lagged in the parade, Sunny bounded back to the baby, staying with him, nudging him, as if he were a baby sheep straggling behind.

Sophy

Sophy wasn't surprised the children and the dog had taken to Caleb so fast. He was a good man. She'd known enough bad men in her past to know the difference. Here she was totally vulnerable. A widow with helpless children. Out in the middle of the prairie, miles from anyone else. No law of any kind.

There were a thousand ways he could have taken advantage of her, but he hadn't.

Maybe God had sent her a blessing after all. She hugged that thought to her.

Chapter 5

After two weeks, Caleb decided something had to be done. Sophy had not only taken him up on his offer to help, she'd decided to give it all to him. He'd seen people suffer from grief. His mother had been much the same way when Grandma died. She'd withdrawn into her own world and let everyone else take care of her household.

He couldn't remember how long that went on with his ma. He'd only been seven but he'd missed his mother's attention. Far as he could remember it went on until Pa had a talk with her. Maybe it was his own fault for volunteering to take care of the children and the chores for a while, but he'd been thinking of a day or two.

Surely she'd understand he couldn't keep it up. The wheat ripening in the fields had to be bundled and after that the new fields had to be backset in preparation for the next year. And he wasn't as experienced as Martin. He didn't

Sophy

know how to handle oxen, which he knew were quite different than horses. As it was, he had to get up an hour earlier to take care of the stock, get the breakfast ready and prepare the children for the day.

She was going to have to take care of the children. Not only did he not have time to give them the proper attention, they needed their mother.

Sophy seemed not to see her children's needs. She sat with her knitting or stood, staring out the window. If she even got out of bed at all. Sleeping was probably good for her, but if she stayed in bed all day, she was neglecting her children. And he was no substitute. Already Heidi was asking why Ma wasn't fixing her mush. Why she didn't take them into the garden? Why she didn't read a bedtime story?

He poured out corn for the hogs. There was another chore waiting for him. The hog killing should take place at the first cold snap, the meat dressed, smoked, and stored in the smoke house. There would be too much pork for Sophy's small family, so she could sell the bulk at Grand Forks or the little river town of St. Andrews even. Had she gone over her accounts since Martin died?

That was probably the last thing on her mind. He washed up at the well and stomped into the house to alert her of his presence. She was sitting in the rocking chair with her knitting, though her hands weren't moving. He crossed the room and stood so his shadow fell over her. She didn't move.

"Sophy, we need to talk after supper."

She nodded to show him she heard.

"I'll get supper for us," he said, "and after you or me put the children down to sleep, we'll go out to sit on the benches just to look at the stars. The skies have been magnificent the last few days." Would she take the hint about putting the children to bed?

She drew in a deep breath. "I know I've been expecting you do everything—taking advantage of you. You have your own work to do. I'll start doing my part." A little laugh escaped her lips. "I've just been so tired. But I know I have to snap out of it or I'm going to run you off. You can't do the farm work and watch the children, too."

"Are you trying to run me off?"

Her head snapped to attention and her gaze studied him. "No, I need you...the children need you, and I'm going to share the proceeds of the wheat sale with you—at least half."

He supposed in her way, she thought she'd be paying him well for his work. It wasn't that. Her children needed her attention. "I have a stew simmering. It'll do for tonight, but we'll finish the bread with supper and I can't make bread." He'd found strips of smoked beef in the spring house and on his way back to the house, pulled carrots, potatoes, and tomatoes from the

Sophy

garden. So many of the tomatoes had gone bad on the vine. If Sophy had been in her right mind, she'd have canned them. He could see her pantry was well stocked with her canned vegetables. Canning was beyond him.

"I can make johnnycake, but the kids would like your bread better." He turned to go, then glanced over his shoulder. "We'll talk about…everything…tonight."

Both Heidi and Marty were good about going to sleep after supper, and after getting them tucked in, Caleb went in search of Sophy. He found her already sitting on the outside bench, staring at the sky. He took a moment to study her profile in the moonlight, the drape of hair over her forehead, the tilt of her nose, the curve of her lips, the slope of her neck. Martin was right. She was a beautiful woman.

He'd like to build her a real porch and make a couple of rockers to put on it. If only he had his carpenter tools with him, but even if he had them, he didn't have the wood. Nor the time.

The full moon had just cleared the tree line to the east and its soft light had cast a soft glow over the yard. Above them, the Milky Way and a million other stars twinkled. Sophy's roses and lilacs scented the air, adding to the dreamy atmosphere. The crickets' song played as Caleb sat on the adjacent bench. "Pretty out tonight."

"It is. Do you suppose Martin is somewhere up there looking down on us?"

"I couldn't say, but I've read enough of my Bible to know it's a wonderful place of peace and joy. If our loved ones could see how we're suffering, I don't think they'd be happy."

She said nothing, but he could hear her soft sigh. He cleared his throat. "Sophy, if it's all right with you, beginning tomorrow, I'd like to have supper a little earlier so I could read some to Heidi before she goes to bed. I brought some books from my ma's library and a couple of them are for children."

"It's all right with me. I'd like to listen in myself."

It was the answer he'd wanted. "Of course, you could listen in while you rock Marty. It'll be a treat for him to be rocked to sleep. Holding him will be a treat for you, too." Caleb caught the look of confusion cross her features and added, "If you'd rather do your needlework while I read a passage from the Bible after the children go to sleep, that'd be okay, too. But my pa always wanted us together when he read the Bible. and it never failed to make us feel good—made our sleep more peaceful."

And the Lord's words might comfort Sophy more than he could.

She shifted and turned her gaze away from him. "Martin read a passage often—not every night—some nights he was just too tired. Martin was a strong believer and I was, too, I thought."

"But now?"

Sophy

"I don't believe God struck Martin dead, you understand. As you said, accidents happen to good people and bad."

"Yeah, like Jesus said, God sends his rain to the just and unjust. But since God knows the future of us all, He'll know when we die. He knows how we'll turn out when we're born, well, even before we born." He'd never really thought of it before, but now he'd said it, he realized that was always what he'd believed. Even now, God knew when he'd die. The important thing was for him to make every day count.

Lord, help me find the words to comfort Sophy. "Don't make it any easier for us when someone we love dies, even knowing they're in a better place and we'll see them again." He stretched his legs out. "It takes a long time to mourn, but life goes on for those of us left behind." He hoped something he said might bring her comfort. Grief could either draw one closer to God, or farther apart.

Her head fell forward and she stared at her hands in her lap.

Since he thought he was getting through to her, he lowered his voice and added, "Things have to be done, especially for the children. You've lost your husband, but they've lost their father, and…you've been neglecting them." That sounded harsh and he hoped she didn't take offense. "I know how you're hurting, Sophy, and I think it's worse for you because you didn't get a chance to say good-bye to Martin."

Elaine Manders

He straightened, pulling his feet under the bench, hoping he was saying the right things. "If you'd like, I'll take you to Grand Forks to visit Martin's grave. It might give you some comfort—some closure."

Her head came up, a spark of light showing in her eyes—light such as he hadn't seen since he'd brought her the terrible news. "I'd like that, but...how?" The light faded as quickly as it had come. "We have to bundle the wheat. The threshers will be here next week."

Added to that, he had to backset the new field, and she had to start canning vegetables and berries. And they both had to pay more attention to the children. "It won't take the threshers but a day or two, then we'll go. With both horses and a light load, it won't take but four days going and coming. That's not much time lost, and we can make up for lost time."

"Yes, I want to go. I have to go." He heard a choke in her voice as she bowed her head again. Nothing else but a soft sniff told him she was silently weeping.

He felt so helpless. She needed a friend, a lady friend who'd walked the same journey and could give her solid advice. He was a friend, for sure, but circumstances made things difficult. How could he feel what she did? Yet, his conscience kept reminding him he was all she had.

Watching her shoulders shake, he slid closer to her and awkwardly put his arm over

Sophy

her back. "I'm sorry, Sophy. Things will get better in time." He rubbed circles on her back and inched his fingers up around her shoulders. So thin her shoulders were. She was so fragile, like an injured bird needing his touch, but he feared his touch might do more harm than good.

A tear fell on his shirt, and he watched it spread as the night crowded around them.

Then she surprised him by shifting on the bench and hiding her face on his chest. He wrapped both arms around her and rested his chin on the top of her head. This was the best way to comfort her. Talk wasn't enough.

Her sobs quieted quickly and she sat back. He took his handkerchief and blotted her face. She sniffed and her lips tipped up in a slight smile. "I'm better now. I want to go look in on Heidi and Marty." Standing, she grabbed the door handle and waited moments to steady herself.

Caleb shot to his feet and opened the door for her. "Thank you," she said. "You can get back to the fields tomorrow. I'll take care of the house from now on…and…I'll have supper waiting by seven o'clock."

He watched her disappear into the house. Thoughts of Sophy stayed in his head all night, and sleep evaded him. He chided himself for letting his mind wander. He couldn't allow himself to have feelings for Sophy. She was in deep mourning for her husband and would be for a long time. But as he plumped the pillow and turned over on his side, he couldn't help thinking of how good she felt in his arms.

Chapter 6

True to her word, Sophy ran him out of her kitchen the next day, but he still worried about her. She seemed to be determined to make up for lost time, working faster than a locomotive—canning, tanning, milking. She refused to let him do any of the household chores. He didn't know if she was trying to prove she didn't need his help, or if keeping busy kept her mind off her loss.

Trouble was her spirit was still lackluster, and she didn't take time to spend any fun time with the children.

Heidi came to him to complain. "Cabub, will you tell Ma you don't want flapjacks and bacon again? She'll make fried chicken for you, and maybe cake."

He stopped hammering the plowshare and squatted down to the little girl's level. "Your ma has a lot to do right now, canning and all. She'll be through with that in a week or two, then she'll cook those good meals like she used to. You can help her by watching Marty."

Heidi's face fell. "I get tired of watching Marty," she whined. "He doesn't know how to do anything, and he pulls my doll's hair out."

Caleb rubbed his nose with the back of his hand. "That is a problem. How would you like for me to build you a swing? I could rig up the ropes to an old crate and both you and Marty could swing. I'll push you every day after lunch. I'll put another swing beside the crate with a flat wood seat, so you can swing yourself."

He didn't really have time to build them a swing. There were no trees big enough. He'd have to sink a couple of logs with a beam running across the top. He'd have to brace the logs to make them steady. The lumber left over from the corral would serve the purpose. It would mean a lot to the children. They stayed inside too much.

When they were outside, Sunny played with them. She'd make a good guard dog if he had time to train her to guard the children. That way, Sophy might let them stay outside while she was working inside. She refused to allow Sunny indoors, though Heidi begged and Marty cried. That was all right. His ma was the same way.

The dog stayed with him in the barn, and though all the other animals did their business in their stalls, Caleb made Sunny go outside. She

Sophy

was the right age to house-break, and she'd live inside his house whenever he had time to build it.

Right now, he had to spend every waking hour bundling the wheat, readying it for the threshers, who waited for no man. It was a monotonous job--bundling the wheat for the threshers—down one row and up the other.

He was out of practice with the scythe. Last year he could've out-performed his brother Barth. Over the past few months, he'd let his muscles get soft. He straightened and lifted the wide brim of his hat with his left hand while wiping the sweat off his face with his right sleeve. This labor was deciding him to farm only enough to prove up his land. The rest would be used for pastures for his draft horses and mules, maybe even oxen. As he yielded the scythe to fell the next wheat stalks, he heard a rustling behind him followed by Sophy's screams.

With Marty anchored on her hip, Sophy held him with one arm, while she ran through the wheat, pushing it out of the way with her other arm as if she were swimming. He dropped the scythe and met her, taking Marty to allow her to catch her breath.

She reached out to grab ahold of Caleb's shoulder. "Heidi is missing." She heaved another breath. "I can't find her anywhere." Her choked words spewed from her mouth.

Caleb took off running to the house, Marty screaming at the top of his lungs and reaching back for his mother. Poor baby didn't know what was happening, but he knew his ma was frantic, and that was enough to upset him, too.

It took Sophy a minute to catch up with Caleb, who scurried toward the back of the house, Sunny at his heels. There were few places to hide around the backyard, but this was Heidi's favorite place to play.

Sophy took Marty from him. "I've looked all over the inside and out—twice."

"The barn?" Caleb was ready to take off.

"I looked there, too." Sophy's voice trembled. "She's never done anything like this."

"Let's look again," Caleb said. "Did you look in the loft?"

"No, she couldn't get up there."

Caleb wouldn't put it past the rambunctious little girl. But after covering every square inch of the property, house and barn, and yelling Heidi's name until he was hoarse, he had to admit she wasn't there. Now he was almost as frantic as Sophy. A child couldn't just disappear into thin air.

"Where did you last see her?" He should've asked that first.

"I was hanging out the wash, and Heidi was running between the sheets, playing boo with Marty. After I got the last of the clothes up, I called for her to follow me, but she didn't answer. When I looked for her, she was gone."

Sophy

Sophy's voice rose with each word until she was shrieking.

Caleb hugged both Sophy and Marty, who was still yelling, his face red and tears staining his ruddy cheeks. "We're going to find her. She couldn't have gone far." But as he looked out at the open prairie—to that land he'd claimed—his heart froze. The grass was taller than Heidi. She could be anywhere in a three-hundred-and-sixty-degree radius.

He'd heard stories of small children getting lost in the prairie grass and the remains not found until months later, if at all. If they couldn't find the child before dark, the chances pf finding her plunged to almost nothing. Coyotes, wolves, and even smaller animals could attack a child and drag her off. Even those varmints from far away could smell their prey for miles.

Even as the thought hit him, Sunny loped toward the front the yard, stopped and ran back to circle them. "Where was Sunny when Heidi went missing?"

Sophy's wailing stopped and she stared wide-eyed. "I don't know." They both stared at the frolicking dog.

Caleb grabbed Sunny's scruff. "Hey, girl, where did Heidi go?"

Sunny licked his hand and gazed at him with begging brown eyes. Caleb's gaze lifted to Sophy. "It rained last night. I should be able to find her prints, and wherever they end, we'll let Sunny take the lead.

Hope flooded Sophy's face, and trust shone in her eyes. Marty had quieted and even he gazed at Caleb like he trusted him to find his sister. Caleb hoped their trust was in God, because they wouldn't be able to find Heidi without His help.

Small footprints churned up most of the yard because Heidi was an active child. Caleb admitted he wasn't a very good tracker, and it was hard to distinguish where those small, bare feet were going. They circled the backyard and house, widening the circle to include the front yard, barn and corral. Sunny followed, sniffing at their heels.

The sun had reached the three-o'clock position in the cloudless blue sky. Caleb and Sophy had forgotten about the noon meal, but Marty fussed, patting his tummy. "Ungee. Ungee." Sophy ignored his whining.

Caleb straightened from his hunched position. "You can take him inside and feed him. I'll call you if I've found her tracks."

Sophy looked torn. She blew out a sigh and nodded, then trotted back to the house.

"Bring a pot and spoon to clang," Caleb called after her. The wind was against them, and would make it hard for Heidi to hear them calling her name.

Caleb found it easier to track without Sophy

Sophy

pressing in on him. Her terror was so great, it was like a heavy weight slowing him down. Sunny, too, was less distracted and began sniffing the ground in front of Caleb.

They were at the edge of the prairie now at the point where his property adjoined Sophy's broken land and fewer footprints marred the ground. Caleb froze. There in the soft soil was the clear print of a little bare foot from the heel to the toes. *Thank you, Lord.* "Heidi," he yelled loud enough to raise a flock of prairie chickens fifty yards away.

Sunny stopped at the print and sniffed. Caleb dropped to his knees, laying his hand on the dog's neck. "Heidi. Find Heidi." He doubted Sunny had a drop of hound in her, but she seemed to understand. She lifted her head, staring out at the high grass, blowing in waves. It had already turned tan and would make good hay if he had time to harvest it.

He glanced back, relieved to find Sophy crossing the yard. She'd donned the straps of the contraption he'd fashioned to hold Marty in place, freeing her hands to hold the pot and spoon. He didn't want to distract Sunny by calling to Sophy, so he gestured her to come on, and she broke into a run that swung Marty from side to side.

Before she reached him, Sunny set off at a trot, blending into the grass. Sophy would have to catch up. He couldn't wait. He had to follow the dog or lose sight of her.

Sunny barked. Had she found Heidi, or was she just chasing a rabbit? Caleb's chest squeezed with both hope and fear. One thing he vowed. He wouldn't stop searching for that precious little girl until he found her. He'd stay out here in the grass with Sunny all night, if necessary.

Sophy's labored breathing alerted him she was closing in.

His heart dropped when Sunny came back and stared at him like asking what to do next. Then he heard something blown in by the stiff wind, a sound soft as a sigh. "Sunny." Heidi's tiny voice brought tears to his eyes. Then again. "Sunny. Cabub." No, he wasn't imagining it. Heidi would be able to see him even if he couldn't see her.

He raised his arm, gesturing to Sophy to follow. "Found." Was there any more beautiful word in the English language?

Sunny scampered back to Heidi, Caleb right on her tail. A shaking of the grass that couldn't be caused by the wind showed him where the child was even before Sunny reached her.

"Cabub, I got losted." Heidi's sweet little face was blotched red and tear-stained.

He scooped her up and kissed her cheek before handing her to her mother. Sophy's tears mingled with her daughter's and her son's howls. Caleb extracted Marty and bounced him while Sophy kissed Heidi, every inch of her, from the top of her head to the bottom of her

Sophy

little, ant-bitten feet.

Caleb strapped Marty to his chest and plucked up the pot and spoon Sophy had dropped. They hadn't been needed, after all. *Praise God.*

"Are you hurt, sweetie?" Sophy asked, examining her child, her voice cracking.

"Ants bit me and I couldn't find you, Ma. I couldn't find Cabub, either."

Caleb couldn't resist, reaching out to brush Heidi's damp hair from her face. "Why did you come out in the grass, little bit?"

"I saw a rabbit. It was trying to eat our carrots, and Ma said she'd make me mittens with a rabbit skin."

"You can't catch a rabbit, darling," Sophy said, giving her another squeeze. "They're too fast, but I promise to make those mittens before winter."

They'd been walking and it seemed in a much shorter time, they stepped out into the yard. "I called you, Ma, over and over again."

"I know, sweetie. We were all searching for you."

As they approached the house, Heidi looked back at Caleb. "I prayed for Jesus to send you to get me so Ma wouldn't be worried." Her gaze then dropped to the dog tagging at his side. "But Jesus sent me Sunny."

No one could argue with that, so everyone, even Marty, fell silent as they made their way to the house. Caleb opened the door for Sophy, who still carried Heidi hugged to her side, but before entering, she pointed a finger at Sunny. "That dog is welcome in this house anytime she wants to come in."

Just like that, Sunny had a new home, and Caleb promised himself he'd take the time to train the dog to guard the children as if they were sheep. They had plenty to thank God for tonight, he and Sophy. The little lost lamb had been found.

No one would be missing at the table tonight. Sophy would not be weeping for another loss.

Chapter 7

It was customary to provide a midday meal for the threshing crew. Sophy had cooked for them the year before and every crumb was devoured by the six hungry men. She planned to have more this year. Ham, baked chicken, pots of potatoes, turnips, carrots, and beans, two loaves of bread, and three pies.

By the time she had the food laid out on the saw horse tables Caleb had set up, sweat was running down her back and her face flamed from hovering over a hot stove all morning. It was all worth it to have the threshers, with their twelve-mule team and steam engine, fill bag after bag of raw grain.

She didn't know how much the final bale count was, but it had to be much more than last year. She didn't even know the price of wheat or how much money was in the bank. Martin had taken care of all that. Another task for her to learn. Another thing to ask Caleb about.

She rolled her shoulders before drawing the water to wash all the dishes left after the big meal. The work never ended, and she didn't know what she'd have done without Caleb. She refused to even think about next year. He would likely have his own farm to worry about. Very possibly, a wife. She didn't know why that should sadden her. He'd spoken of a woman waiting for him back in Illinois when he'd first arrived.

Clarise. He'd intended to return home and spend the winter preparing for their wedding next spring. Then they'd return to build a home. Start a small ranch. Grow a family.

Instead, he'd felt obligated to stay and help her bring in the harvest, then get through the winter. She was a burden to him. Sophy pressed down that sick feeling in the pit of her stomach where a mass of jealousy was growing.

She'd insist he leave next spring. Caleb deserved a good woman, and she prayed he'd find happiness with Clarise.

Somehow, she'd make it alone. She had to for Heidi and Marty. She was grateful to Caleb for training Sunny to guard the children and giving the dog to them. At first, she wouldn't let them go outside unless she was with them. But after she saw how the dog herded them like sheep, her worries eased.

It was funny, really, if one of the children got out of the bounds Caleb had set, Sunny would block that child, barking her head off.

Sophy

Sophy knew she'd hear the bark no matter where she was on the property.

Caleb had house-broken the dog, and she slept in the children's room. Always on guard. They would start out for Grand Forks tomorrow morning and Sunny would go with them. Caleb would leave extra water and food for the stock. The chickens would stay enclosed in the coop in hopes they'd be here when they returned.

It was always a risk leaving the farm without anyone on site for four days, but she and Martin had done it on more than one occasion. They'd been blessed to find everything as they left it so far. Every few weeks during the summer, travelers would stop for a meal or a place to stay the night. Usually these were families who meant no harm.

She hadn't thought about it, but they were past due for visitors. Six weeks had passed since the last traveler stopped by. Actually, no one had visited the farm since Caleb arrived. Would anyone pass by while they were away?

As if to answer her question, they'd only been traveling the well-beaten road to Grand Forks for a little more than two hours when a prairie schooner appeared on the horizon.

"It's a family, or at least a couple," Caleb said. "Since they have a team of oxen, they're looking to settle."

Sophy shifted the sleeping Marty in her lap. "I hope they settle near us—if they're nice." Most of the settlers passed them by, because the area she and Martin had claimed was so far from a town, and the forest was thin and farther away from the best farm land.

Caleb met her gaze. "It is desolate, but I heard there are more immigrants coming from Europe in the next few years. Before the turn of the century, all the land will be claimed."

"True. The Muntz family that moved out from the section you claimed were immigrants. I think if they could've spoken English, we might have become friends."

The covered wagon coming toward them was much slower than their team, but when they got within hollering distance, the couple yelled and waved their arms. Sophy and Caleb returned their greetings. "Looks like a friendly sort."

Heidi poked herself between them. She'd been playing with Sunny in the back of the wagon. "Who is that, Ma?"

"I don't know. Recon we'll see in a minute. You want to sit up here?"

In answer the little girl scrambled over the seat, scooting as close to Sophy as she could. Sunny stuck her head over Caleb's shoulder and barked.

Caleb reined in and the driver of the approaching wagon did the same. "Good-day," the man said. "I'm Charles Huffington and this is my wife, Alma."

Sophy

"Good-day." Caleb gave his name and added Sophy's, the children's, and even the dog's.

"You're not married?" Alma Huffington asked. There was a note of censure in her voice.

Sophy decided to let Caleb do the talking. Traveling with a man not related might seem strange to the Huffingtons, but Caleb hid nothing. "We're neighbors. Mrs. Schneider is a widow and these are her children."

Sunny barked and Caleb laughed. "We share the dog."

Three youngsters popped their heads out of the canvas covered wagon, obviously curious about the dog. Mr. Huffington hushed them and fell into a discussion with Caleb about land claims and the advantages of settling close to the river.

Sophy felt the woman's gaze on her and smiled. Mrs. Huffington was older but not by much. Her children were quite a bit older than Heidi, and Sophy couldn't help thinking the woman had married a widower and gained three children.

"Exactly where did you settle? Is it good land? Can you see the river from your home? Have you proved your land yet?" All of these questions came from Mrs. Huffington like bullets from a six-shooter.

"We'll prove up next year...at least I will. My late husband and I had already built our house and outbuildings, and cultivated the required number of acres, but I'll have to wait another year to meet the time requirement."

Mrs. Huffington shook her head in sympathy. "Seems unfair. If you've done all that's necessary, why do you have to wait?"

"Because some people just up and abandon their claims even after building their house and bringing in a cash crop." Sophy saw the sincere interest in the woman's eyes. She wanted assurance that she and her husband could make it out here in this harsh land. In all honesty, Sophy couldn't give her any assurance. "A couple of immigrants stayed with a claim next to us for two years and left. They didn't realize how hard it is."

"Oh, my." Mrs. Huffington pulled a face. "Maybe they weren't up to the hard work, or prepared. Charles and I have been planning this move for a year now. We've read all the information."

"That was wise." There was a lot of information distributed by government and commercial concerns, but, in Sophy's estimation, they exaggerated the favorable points, and failed to talk about the hard work and sacrifice required.

The Huffingtons moved on and Caleb said, "Maybe they'll settle in our area."

"Maybe, but I probably talked Mrs. Huffington out of it by telling her how terrible

Sophy

those first years are."

He chuckled, a pleasant sound that blended in with the rushing wind. "Never hurts to tell the truth."

"When are we getting to the town, Cabub?" Heidi's tone held that whine that said she was bored. Sophy and Martin had always started out for Grand Forks at night. That way the children could sleep the first twenty-four-hour leg of the journey. Then they'd spend most of the daylight hours in town doing whatever business and shopping they had, returning the next night.

Caleb probably hadn't thought of how fussy the children could get, and she hadn't thought to tell him.

"We've got a ways to go yet, little bit," Caleb said. "We'll camp out tonight and get to town early tomorrow." He was always so patient with the children, more so than Martin, if Sophy were honest about it. Actually, Caleb was patient with her. He was just a patient man, and she'd never seen him anxious. No, she'd seen him under stress when Heidi went missing. He'd tried to control his emotions to calm her, but she'd seen the fear in his eyes. The love he already had for her little girl.

"I don't know when tomorrow is," Heidi said.

Caleb threw a glance for help at Sophy. "Tomorrow is the next day."

"It's when the sun comes up again," Caleb

added. "The Indians say it's one sleep away."

"Oh, I know now. Cabub, that man in the wagon had a long beard. Why don't you have a long beard?" Heidi stroked his face, her little hand moving from his cheek to his chin. She got up on her knees and ran her fingers through his hair, twirling it into curls like she did to Marty's hair.

Sophy couldn't help the envy that fell like an unexpected memory. She missed the feel of a man. The smell, the touch. She wondered if she should stop her daughter. Heidi had a million questions. Martin got annoyed by Heidi's constant chatter.

But Caleb seemed to give great thought to answering. "I just don't like a beard, so I cut it off. Some men like the look of a beard, or they don't like to take the time to shave."

"My pa had a short beard," Heidi said. "Marty will have a beard like him when he grows up. Will I have a beard when I grow up?"

Caleb chuckled. "Let's hope not."

Sophy smiled. The first honest smile that had curved her lips since Martin died. "Heidi, you know you'll be a woman when you grow up and women don't have beards." She lifted Marty, who was squirming and getting hard to hold still. "I'm going to put Marty in the back with Sunny. You'll have to get back there to make sure he doesn't fall out."

Heidi's head fell back and she closed her

Sophy

eyes in that long-suffering look she gave when she didn't want to do something.

Caleb took notice. "Go ahead and do as your mother says. Your ma told me your birthday is next week. You be good, and we'll go ahead and celebrate when we get to Grand Forks, We'll have a birthday dinner for you before we come back with cake just for you."

"A cake, just for me?"

"We'll all have a piece, but you can have the first slice."

Heidi clapped her hands. "I'll be this many on my birthday." She held up her hand, showing four fingers. "See when I hide my thumb, it leaves my four fingers. When I'm five—"

"Heidi, get on back there and play with your brother." Marty was setting up a squall, sure to turn into a shriek that might startle the horses.

With an exaggerated sigh, Heidi jumped into the back.

Sophy shared a smile with Caleb. "I apologize for Heidi's annoyance. Sometimes she behaves like a pesky fly, and thank you for offering her a birthday party. She's never had one."

"She doesn't bother me a bit. I probably help her remember her pa—like she's searching for a substitute."

"Maybe," Sophy said. Was that what she was doing, too? Searching for a substitute for

Martin? "You're the only other man she's known. Thank you for taking up time with her—and Marty. It helps me a lot."

He scrubbed a hand through his hair. "I'm just doing my Christian duty."

That hit her like a dash of cold water, though she didn't know why. Yes, she did. In the two months since Caleb had come, she'd developed feelings for him—feelings unseemly for a new widow. But already memories of Martin were growing dim. Maybe after she visited his grave…

Even now, she stared at Caleb's profile, lingering over the way his shoulder muscles bunched when he handled the reins. The way he held his head high with his hat pulled low over his forehead. The way his chestnut hair curled around his ear. Every quirk and movement of his face had become dear.

She forced her eyes away to gaze at the endless prairie. Caleb didn't belong to her, and never would. She'd have to remember that.

He belonged to Clarise.

Chapter 8

The next day they rolled into Grand Forks as the sun crested the horizon, creating such a glorious display of gold and rose it almost took Sophy's breath away. When was the last time she'd taken the time to watch a sunrise? Chores ate up time on the farm. All she could think of, even now, was the work not getting done. Only for Martin would she have pulled herself away from duty.

Caleb reined in the horses next to a decorative iron fence with an open gate. The children were in back, still sleeping. "I'll leave you here and take the young'uns with me to the feed store," he said. "I think Heidi is too young to visit a grave, but I'll leave that up to you. I'll be back in an hour. Will that give you enough time?"

She couldn't utter a word, but managed to nod an affirmative. No, she wasn't prepared to explain to Heidi that her father lay in the ground here.

Caleb helped her down. "You'll find Martin's grave in the back to the right, near a cottonwood tree. Look for the granite headstone."

Martin's grave. The words jolted her and she was grateful for Caleb's support. "You bought a headstone?"

"I ordered it, and after two months, it ought to be there. Are you going to be all right?"

His furrowed brows showed his concern and brought a smile she didn't feel to her face. "Yes, I'll be fine." She glanced at her lapel watch. "I'll meet you here in an hour."

She didn't wait for him to drive away, but stiffened her spine and strode through the gate. Weaving around the right side of the grounds to keep from trampling the grave sites, she made her way to the back. She'd worn her dark blue traveling dress of summer linen, and the morning chill forced her to pull her shawl tighter around her shoulders. She spotted the large cottonwood, and her feet dragged like they were shackled with iron chains. Until now, she'd held onto the illusion that it was all a mistake and Martin would show up any day.

The headstone was beautiful. She ran her fingers over the lettering. Caleb had told her the riverboat captain had given him Martin's birthdate. Under that date, and the date of death, chiseled into the stone were the words,

Sophy

Beloved Husband of Sophy.

She couldn't help but smile at that. It was true.

Dropping to her knees, she glanced around to make sure she was alone, though at this time of morning, it wasn't likely that anyone would be here. Not a sound broke the stillness, even the birds had quieted.

The silence begged her to speak aloud. "Martin, we miss you so much." She sniffed. "But I've come to say good-bye. I know you're in a better place, but the emptiness you've left leaves a big hole." She pushed back, resting on her legs. "I wished your...your remains could've been buried on our land, but Caleb couldn't...it was too long."

She didn't know why it was necessary to explain for Caleb. He did as much—more—than could have been expected. "I come to Grand Forks twice a year, so I'll be visiting each time. I promise not to forget. I still love you, Martin. If you can't hear me where you are, I pray God will let you know that." The tears that she'd managed to hold back until now flowed. "No one can ever take your place in my heart."

She carried on her monologue, telling him about the children, everything she could remember. All the little things she knew he'd enjoy hearing. She told of the harvest, the best yet. "Thank you for sending Caleb. I couldn't have done everything without him."

Elaine Manders

It occurred to her she mentioned Caleb a lot, but Martin had to know. "I'm developing feelings for him, Martin, even after two months. Many would think that's disloyal to you, but it isn't, and I can't help thinking he cares for the children...and me. I just...just had to tell you because I've always told you everything that's on my heart."

Then she remembered something else funny Heidi had said and the way Marty was taking his first steps. "They've grown so much, Martin. You'd be proud of them. I promise to keep the farm and make it grow like we'd planned, to leave it to them."

"They miss their pa, and...and they need a father. Right now, they look to Caleb to do all the things you did for them, all the things you taught them."

She swiped the tears from her face and more fell. "I won't let them forget you. You'll always be their pa."

The rumble of wagon wheels snagged her attention. Caleb had returned. Had she been talking for an hour? She opened her lapel to confirm the time, and sure enough, her time with Martin had come to an end. Caleb had said she could stay as long as she wished, but she'd said it all.

Her heart felt suddenly light. "I'm not sure what to do, Martin. You'll always be my first love, but for the first time, I realize I must be open to find a husband and a father for Heidi

Sophy

and Marty. I can't depend on Caleb forever. He has plans to marry someone his family chose for him. But sometime in the future—two or three years, perhaps—there will be someone, I hope. I'll be praying for that because I know that's what you would want."

She lowered herself across the grave's granite slab, as if giving Martin a final hug. "Every time I'm in Grand Forks, I'll come by and tell you how we're doing. Good-bye and thank you for giving me seven years of happiness."

Before she reached the wagon, Heidi yelled, standing on the seat beside Caleb. "Ma! Ma! Cabub gave me a new doll for my birthday. Come see, Ma. She has a real hair and rosy cheeks."

Caleb jumped down to help her onto the seat. "You spoil her," she chided. She knew Caleb was using his hard-earned savings to put into his homestead. He was delaying the work he should have been doing for his own place to help her with the harvest and prepare for winter. All he'd taken from her so far was meals and a place to sleep in the barn.

She'd offered him a portion of the harvest, but he'd refused.

As she'd been talking to Martin at the gravesite, she'd realized she hoped he'd wait for her. Give her time to prepare her heart for another love.

No. She couldn't do that. He deserved a

helpmate now to make a home for a family of his own. A farm and the horse ranch he wanted. His own children. A future with Sophy as a neighbor and nothing more.

But could she stand back and watch him return with a bride? Could she keep her feelings to herself as another woman went into his arms? A woman who would bear his children? Children who would take his time from Heidi and Marty?

It was the right way for it to happen. The Good Lord knew it was right.

But her heart still ached.

Chapter 9

A smoke spiral appeared as they crested the rise that marked the mile to home. "Looks like the Huffingtons decided to settle next to our claims," Caleb said. At least he hoped it was the Huffingtons. Sometimes a vacant homestead would attract squatters, and the homeowners would find their claim taken over upon their return. They wouldn't invade Sophy's place, since it was clearly a settled claim. But his claim looked, and, so far, was, abandoned.

Sophy got to the edge of the seat and used her hand to shade her eyes. "I do hope so. I've never had a lady neighbor who could speak English."

Caleb glanced from her white-knuckled grip on the wagon seat to the eager look on her face. This woman was amazing. She was a real trail blazer. How lonely she must have been, working with nothing but hope and her husband's love. Nonetheless, she'd made a

Elaine Manders

comfortable home out of nothing but sheer will and the earth.

Did she trust in God? He still couldn't answer that question, though she'd sat through his reading of the Scripture most nights he'd been here.

She kept her thoughts locked tightly inside her.

"How many children did they have?" Sophy asked. "Five, wasn't it?"

"That we saw." He gave her a smile and a wink.

A light chuckle escaped her lips as she relaxed. "I noticed Mrs. Huffington was a heavy-set woman with a thick waist. She might be in the family way again, although her baby couldn't have been over six months old."

"True." They'd become comfortable with each other—he and Sophy. Comfortable enough to discuss any topic, almost like brother and sister, but he found it hard to think of Sophy as he did his sisters.

He slowed Sibbie, his mare and Spike, the name he'd given his new stallion, as the wagon rolled across Sophy's yard. On the far side, the whole Huffington clan trekked toward them. Sunny caught wind of these new people and started barking. Caleb unfastened the dog's leash and Sunny tore off to inspect the new people.

Sophy

Charles Huffington came first, his hand outstretched to Caleb. "Jack and Ben can take care of your horses and rig and Jane can help with the little ones so the ladies can get acquainted."

Caleb assumed Jack and Ben were the two older boys who looked to be maybe twelve and thirteen. Jane was probably a little older. "I appreciate it," Caleb said, grasping the man's hand.

"We kept a check on your stock, too," Charles said. "I hope you don't mind, but we milked the cow and used the milk."

"Sophy thought Lou would go dry." The other cow was due to drop her calf before Thanksgiving, or so he and Sophy had judged.

"If Lou's the cow's name, she hasn't gone dry yet. She put out enough for my young'uns."

Alma Huffington reached the wagon, a coffee pot held high, her baby riding on her hip. "I thought you folks would like some hot coffee after that long trip."

Sophy handed Marty over to Jane and took the pot. "Thank you. Let's all go in and have a cup." She held the door open for her guests. "You could've come in and used my stove."

"No, we wouldn't think of coming in someone else's house and the owner not there."

"We're living in our wagon while we're here," Charles said. "We'll be leaving when the first snow falls and come back next spring to build our soddy and bust sod."

They all trooped in to Sophy's kitchen and the walls seemed to close in with so many people taking up the space. "That sounds like a sensible plan. Some folks try to live in their wagons through the winter," Caleb said. "Not a good idea."

"I have a room in the loft," Sophy offered. "Some of you could camp out in the parlor. It would be a tight fit, but it'd give you more room than your wagon would."

"What do you think, Charles?" Alma sent a pleading look to her husband.

Charles shook his bushy head. "No, we need to get used to our own land." He laughed. "Besides, we want these folks to become friends as well as neighbors, and the best way to ruin a friendship is crowd them."

Alma looked longingly at Sophy's spacious kitchen, then smiled. "He's right. It's kind of you to offer, but we couldn't put you out." The exchange between the couple told Caleb as good as words that Charles dominated his wife and she didn't particularly like it.

He knew from his talks with Martin, his and Sophy's marriage was nothing like that. They were equally yoked in life. Sophy did her best to please her husband and that made him want to please her. Caleb could only hope for the same type of relationship with his future wife.

Sophy

Sophy asked Caleb to bring in some extra chairs. She'd set mugs around the table for everyone except Lenny, the youngest baby. When he returned, she was pouring coffee—strong for the adults, a watered-down version for the children.

Caleb got the cream from the icebox and the sugar from the pantry. When he set them on the table, Alma caught his eye. "Are you related to Sophy, Mr. Beckham?"

He exchanged a glance with Sophy. The meaning was clear. Alma already knew he and Sophy weren't related. She simply didn't think they were in a proper relationship.

Everyone stared at their mugs, even the children, as metal clinked on china. Stirring her coffee, Sophy spoke. "Alma, Caleb and I aren't related except as brother and sister in Christ, and in that role, he's helped this widow and her children get in our crops and done our chores at the expense of neglecting his own land. He's doing this, not only as his Christian duty, but as a favor to my late husband."

Caleb knew how much Sophy wanted to make friends with Alma, but she'd taken her stand and he admired her for it. Trying to think of a way to soften the stern tone of her words, he added. "May I suggest we all use our first names out here, since we're all going to be friends. No need for formalities as far as I'm concerned." He raised his mug, and thankfully, everyone raised theirs in agreement, although Alma waited to see what Charles would do.

Heidi piped up, "Ma, my new friend, Susie, wants one of my birthday cookies."

Caleb pushed back from the table and caught Sophy's gaze. "I brought them in." He explained to everyone, "Heidi's birthday is next week, and while we were in Grand Forks I promised her a dinner with cake, but we had to leave before the restaurant opened, so I bought a dozen cookies from the bakery. There'll be enough for all of us to have one."

"I'd forgotten about the cookies," Sophy said. "You don't mind sharing with everyone, do you, Heidi?"

Caleb waited to see what the little girl would say, and knowing Heidi, it could be anything. "It's good to share, isn't it, Ma?" When Sophy nodded, Heidi glanced back at Caleb. "Bring all of them, please, Cabub."

He couldn't have been prouder of their Heidi. She was on her best behavior. Before he got to the door, Sophy said, "I'd like to invite you all to Heidi's birthday party next Tuesday."

Alma's hard features loosened into a smile. "Thank you. We'd love to come, and I could come early and help you cook. In fact, anytime you'd like me to help, I'd be glad to."

After they had enjoyed their coffee and cookies, Sophy offered to show Alma the rest of the house. The men followed the older children outside. Charles asked Caleb to show him the

Sophy

stock.

The man was full of questions. "Looks like this cow is ready to drop a calf."

"That's Luce, yes we figure in another month. Good thing since Lou is about dry."

"Did you butcher her calf?"

"No, I think Martin sold it."

After Charles had admired Caleb's horseflesh, he took his red handkerchief and wiped the sweat from his brow. It was a hot day. "Sure is a nice farm. What about you? How much ground to you intend to bust this year?"

"I won't have time to do any more than has already been busted, not this year, anyway." He didn't have to inform Charles about his plans for a horse ranch. Some farmers scoffed at such a notion. A waste of good land, some had said, besides horses or cattle always escaped their barbwire fences and would trample and eat their crops. The contention between farmers and ranchers was worse farther west, but no need to put a bad taste in Charles's mouth. "I'll have to leave before Thanksgiving and not return until April."

Charles's brows reached under the brim of his hat. "What about the stock? What about Sophy? She going with you? Any plans to marry?"

Caleb didn't think the Huffington's friendship had advanced far enough to ask such

"Five dozen," Sophy said. "I have the rest stored in the cellar, but you can have three dozen jars. Just get them as you need them."

"That's too much, surely."

"You're welcome to them. You did most of the work." And anyway, Sophy wouldn't need them. She had pickles left over from last year. Her garden always produced more than she needed. It was good to have neighbors to share with.

Alma ambled to the window and pulled the curtains back. "I feel like we're imposing on you. When we get settled, I'll find some way to pay you back."

When Sophy didn't reply, Alma added, "I see Susie and Heidi with the dog. Wonder where Jane and the babies got off to."

"June fell asleep, so Jane came in and laid her in the cradle. She said she was going to swing Marty on that swing Caleb put up in the backyard. Marty really loves it." Sophy wiped her hands on a dishrag and went to the stove. Everything was a mess and she'd clean up after a cup of coffee. "Sit down and take a breather."

"Thanks, don't mind if I do. I'll have to bring in the wash before dark," Alma laughed. "As you know, I have a lot. That's another thing I have to thank you for. Your well water makes wash day so much easier than hauling water from the river."

"I had to do that the first two years Martin

90

Chapter 10

After a week, the Huffingtons decided to take up Sophy's offer to move in. She wasn't surprised they'd changed their minds. Camping outside and living in a wagon would do that to a settler. Most had no choice, but the Huffingtons did because Sophy followed the golden rule of the settlers—help thy neighbor.

She was glad to have them, and the house wasn't crowded at all. The two older boys slept in the barn with Caleb. Charles, Alma, Jane, and baby June moved into the spacious loft bedroom. Susie moved in with Heidi. Except for the problem of two women running the same kitchen, there were no problems.

Alma set the last of the canned pickles on the table, stepped back and nodded her approval. "That's another dozen jars. How many does that make in all?"

"I appreciate the offer, and I'll talk to Sophy about it."

It wasn't like he hadn't racked his brain for a solution to the problem. Charles was right. Sophy and the children shouldn't be left alone out here through a Dakota winter. His mother—his whole family—would love to have them and they had room. He'd ask, but he knew she'd refuse.

personal questions. He well knew both Charles and Alma thought he and Sophy should get married, but it seemed disrespectful to Martin. He hadn't been dead more than two months. Besides, Sophy would never agree to marry anyone until a proper mourning period had passed. Maybe never. And, then, there was Clarise waiting for him.

"I'd ask Sophy to go with me to visit with my family, but she won't go. She knows there's no one to look after the stock, and the winters can be hard. She knows how hard. She's been through five of them."

Charles shook his head. "That woman can't stay here by herself with those little ones to take care of. If she won't go with you, we'll invite her to go with us."

"You can ask, but she won't leave this farm. I haven't known her long, but long enough to know that."

"Have you asked her?"

"No, but I will. I thought maybe she'd agree for old Ike Rand, who lives in that dug-out by the river, if he'd stay the winter and take care of the stock. He says he goes to stay with his people during the winter but I gather he don't like them much."

"Better ask her soon or you'll find her dead in the spring. Her and the young'uns. All of you can leave with us. Would make it more...respectable...on the trail."

87

and I were here. You have to strain the river water before you wash, and you have to strain it twice to drink." Sophy poured a cup for her friend and herself and went to fetch the cream and sugar.

"I never even thought of the water being dirty. Settling out here isn't for the faint of heart." Alma held her cup daintily for a farmwoman, always with her little finger in the air. She changed the subject abruptly. "Of all my children, I worry about Jane the most."

"Why? She's a lovely young girl."

"Almost a woman. Where is she going to find a husband out here?"

"She won't need one for a couple of years. Other families will move in. One is sure to have a handsome young man."

Alma sighed. "I surely hope so." She set her cup down and narrowed her eyes. "Since you're not interested in Caleb, what do you think of him courting my Jane? She'll be seventeen next year."

Sophy almost strangled on her coffee. She couldn't argue about the age. She and Martin had married when she was seventeen and Martin had been eight years older. That didn't make it right, though. "Caleb is much too old for Jane," she said.

"Just nine years. My grandma was twelve years older than my grandpa. They had a good marriage. Funny thing, she had twelve

Sophy

children—eight survived."

So, Alma had counted up the years. The idea of Caleb being the father of twelve children turned Sophy's stomach. Alma had to put that plan to match him up with Jane to rest now. "Caleb has been courting a lady back in Illinois, where he's from. He expects to get married next spring and bring his bride back with him when he returns."

That didn't deter Alma. "The lady might not wait for him. If he starts noticing Jane, he might take a bride to meet his family next spring."

"I think he's promised to Clarise, though. Her family is friends with his family." That was all Sophy could think to say, but by the look in Alma's eyes, she wouldn't stop her from trying to throw her daughter at Caleb. Sophy would have to warn him.

Baby June's wail saved her from more of Alma's matchmaking talk. "She'll be hungry," Alma said, stretching the kinks out of her neck. "I'll help get supper started when I finish feeding June."

"Thank you. I'll get the bread in the oven while you do that." The women worked well together and, in spite of her romantic notions, Sophy liked Alma, and since the Huffingtons had moved into the house, they no longer bothered her with questions about respectability. She would miss them when they left for the winter.

Everything would be different when the Huffingtons returned next year. They would have their own house a mile away. And Caleb would move into his new house right next door. With his bride. She'd tried to put the thought out of her mind, but it was like a stitch in the side that would disappear, then come back when one least expected it.

She made her way to the front door and stepped outside. Children's laughter floated from the back of the house. While it was annoying to have so many crowded in her house, Sophy enjoyed the freedom of having Alma and her children handy to look after Heidi and Marty.

Bright sunshine enveloped her but a cool wind blew in from the north. She covered her elbows with her hands, wishing she'd snagged her shawl. Winter wasn't far off and as much as she'd miss the Huffingtons company, she'd missed the intimacy of the evenings with just her and Caleb and the children.

She hadn't seen nearly as much of Caleb since the Huffingtons had come and never alone. That was a good way to protect her heart, she told herself. But every time Caleb sent her that half smile he saved just for her, her pulse skittered.

When it had just been the two of them and the children, Caleb would read a story for Heidi and Marty after supper. When they'd gone to bed, he'd read from the Bible while she sat doing

Sophy

her mending or working on the farm accounts. That had been Martin's and her habit, and she'd suggested it.

Their habits had changed when the Huffingtons moved in. They were Christian people and Charles read a Scripture after supper, but that was all he did. He never asked the opinion of the verses, nor given his.

"Hey, you."

Sophy almost jumped out of her skin at the familiar deep voice, maybe because she'd been thinking about Caleb. Lately, his very presence would send a flutter to her stomach, and she chided herself for the reaction. It simply wasn't decent for a widow of a few months to think of a man that way. She had to keep reminding herself of that.

Caleb stood with two fishing poles balanced over his shoulder. "Sorry to startle you. I was wondering if you'd like to go fishing with me. I'd love to have some fresh fried fish for supper."

Fishing? She hadn't gone fishing since Martin— "The boys don't want to go?"

"They're helping their pa out at their campsite. I can fish two poles, but it would be a lot more pleasant to have your company."

Smiling, she squinted to see his form silhouetted against the lowering sunshine. "I'd like that. Just give me a minute to tell Alma and grab my shawl."

Sophy hadn't been to the river in over a year and now the smell hit her first. How would one describe it? Strong. Fishy. Pungent. To her a pleasant smell.

Caleb baited both hooks, although she assured him she wasn't afraid of worms. "I didn't think you would be." His strong, white teeth flashed in a smile. "Are you getting tired of your home being overrun with settlers?"

"No, I've enjoyed having the Huffingtons." She certainly wouldn't complain when they moved into their own house, though. "Are you getting tired of Jack and Jim?"

Caleb threw his line in and sat on the log beside her. "No, they remind me of me and my older brothers. I hope I'm more patient with them than my brothers were." He grinned to show he was teasing.

"The Huffington boys are probably not as annoying as you were to your brothers." She bumped him on the arm. "You already have a bite."

He pulled out a plate-sized perch, a good eating fish. "If we catch seven more of that size, we'll have enough for everyone except the little ones, and they don't eat fish," Sophy said, watching the tip of her pole.

"Why is that?" Caleb dropped his fish into the wire mesh trap he'd brought to hold the fish and anchored it in the little inlet outside the river's stream. "Bones?"

Sophy

"Yes, I could pick the fish off the bones for Heidi but she doesn't like fish."

Caleb dug out another worm from the tin can. "Too bad. Maybe I can show her how to eat fish."

"She'll do anything you suggest. Heidi loves you."

He dropped his line a little farther downstream of Sophy. "I love her. Marty too." He gave her a sidelong glance. "Love their mama, too."

Her heart did a crazy flop until he added, "As a sister in Christ. How much more can one love?" He stared into her eyes, as if wanting an answer. She had none.

That was a hard question because she had to admit she wished for a different kind of love. Again, she chided herself. Martin had been gone barely four months and here she was longing for another husband. No, that wasn't quite true. Not just any husband. She wanted Caleb.

Before she could form an answer, he worked a letter out from his pocket without getting up. "I need your advice on something. This is a letter from my mother, along with two photographs of Clarise. She wants to know which dress I'd prefer for our wedding reception. I don't know how to judge women's dresses. What do you think?"

Sophy lowered her pole to the ground. Securing it under her foot, she accepted the letter with a shaky hand. She'd have liked to shove it unopened back at him, but common courtesy demanded she show some interest.

She opened the pages and gave them a glance before plucking the photographs from the envelope. Both dresses were beautiful, one suitable for an afternoon wedding and the other for evening. The woman who wore them was lovely with expressive eyes and dark hair.

"I know those dresses are both fancy," Caleb said, "but Clarise grew up on a farm and she wants to show out."

Probably the daughter of a gentleman farmer. Both dresses in the photographs were expensive, as was the jeweled necklace around Clarise's neck. Sophy looked down at her faded calico. She'd never be able to afford such fine dresses as Clarise wore.

Caleb was used to fine things, too. He'd grown up the son of a gentleman farmer. Sophy knew he planned to build a fine house. Had already ordered the lumber to build it. He wanted to raise horses, and she had no doubt he'd have a large horse ranch one day—a home befitting Clarise.

"What does your family think of Clarise?"

Caleb laughed, and the sound seemed to ease her raw feelings a bit. "They are so glad I've decided to settle down, they are satisfied. I traveled the west with my older brother who was a circuit preacher. David often visited the dens

Sophy

of iniquity, looking for souls to save, and I made the acquaintance of a number of saloon ladies in that way—much to my mother's consternation. So, she'd be satisfied with any respectable woman."

"Your mother doesn't want you to live out here alone. I wouldn't want that for Heidi or Marty." Her voice strained, maybe revealing too much. Tears burned the backs of her eyes. She noticed her hands. Chapped. Calloused. The nails chipped and broken. At this time of year, freckles would dot her nose and cheeks. She didn't know that for sure because she couldn't remember the last time she'd looked in the mirror. Certainly, she never put her hair up like Clarise. How could she ever think to compete with her?

Fortunately, the end of Caleb's pole dipped, and he turned his attention to the fish he'd snagged. It would give her enough time to get away without revealing her feelings. She laid the letter on the log. "Would you take care of my pole? I'd better get back before Marty wakes from his nap."

Before he had time to stop her, she fled. What was happening to her? The only reason she should care about the type of woman Caleb married was that his wife would be her neighbor. But there were other reasons bringing the tears streaming down her face. And she was honest enough to admit it.

She swiped her face and let the brisk wind

dry her tears before reaching the yard. If there was some way to avoid Alma Sophy would have taken it, but the woman was waiting just inside the door. "You got back quick. Fish not biting?"

"Not for me, but Caleb was pulling them in. We'll be having fish for supper, so I'll bake some cornbread. Since we have that big bowl of beans for canning, we'll cook a potful of them."

Alma gave her a funny look. "Are you all right?"

She forced a toothy grin. "Of course. I'd better see to Marty."

"He woke up while you were gone. I diapered him and gave him to Jane so he could play with the girls."

She had to get away from Alma. "Thank you. I'm going to change out of these fishy smelling clothes." She rushed to her room like a bear was after her.

Closing the door, she fell back against it and closed her eyes. She crossed the room to her desk and, opening the drawer, found Martin's Bible. She hadn't opened it since he died. *Lord, lead me to some answers. I didn't mean to fall in love with Caleb. I haven't really seen much of him since the Huffingtons moved in. How am I to go out there and act like nothing's happened?*

This is the way she prayed, getting away from everything and communing with God through her spirit. But she hadn't done that since Martin died and her effort seemed

Sophy

awkward—like God wasn't listening.

She opened the Bible at the bookmark, the place they'd stopped on the evening before he left for Grand Forks. He'd never returned, but Caleb did. Had she looked on Caleb as a substitute for her husband from the first?

It was easy to do. Caleb was so kind and understanding. A man with a sense of duty, who loved his family, and had plans for the future. Why did she think she was a part of his plans? Because she wanted to. Because he was easy to love.

The answers drifted through her mind one by one as her gaze fell upon the page, at the top, Psalm thirty-seven, beginning with verse three.

Trust in the Lord, and do good. Dwell in the land and feed on His faithfulness.

The words of the psalmist spoke to her. *Delight yourself also in the Lord and He shall give you the desires of your heart.*

The children were coming inside, their childish noise filling the house. Such blessings. Her comfortable home. The promise of neighbors. Caleb. She didn't know where God would lead, but she would wait, thankful for all she had.

Chapter 11

"Well, are you going with us?" The Huffingtons would leave at daybreak tomorrow. Indian summer had reached its peak and the days, as well as the nights forced all of them to wear coats.

Caleb didn't immediately answer Charles's question. He tucked his hat to better shade his eyes, but still had to squint to look west. The sun would soon begin its descent below the horizon. "No, I can't."

Charles chewed on a sprig of grass, how he'd stopped the habit of chewing tobacco. Said Alma would leave him if he didn't. Even Alma had her limits. "Didn't expect you would. Kinda relieves my mind. Just can't leave Sophy and those young'uns alone through the winter." He spit the grass out. "Alma and I were hoping you'd marry her." He chuckled. "Well, actually, Alma wanted to see if you'd take a shine to Jane,

Sophy

but I wasn't for that."

Caleb darted a look at the man, then relaxed. Charles was joking. "No, I don't think that would work."

"If you would marry Sophy, we'd stay here to take care of things until you go into Grand Forks and find a preacher."

This wasn't the first time Caleb had heard the offer. The Huffingtons were good people who cared for their neighbors. He was glad they were staking their claim and returning in the spring. Relieved his mind that they'd be here when he made the trip home.

"No that wouldn't work, either. Sophy's still mourning her husband." This was the argument he'd always given, but this time it sounded a little hollow. Why he didn't explain to Charles that he had a bride waiting for him in Illinois, he didn't know. And he wasn't sure about Sophy's feelings, either.

She had changed. He could tell it in her demeanor and her eyes. She was a woman who accepted Martin's death and was in the process of one preparing to carry on alone. Except—

"Nothing disrespectful in remarrying after a few months when she has to." Charles laughed shortly. "She's a stubborn woman, but no woman, no matter how stubborn, can survive out here alone."

"Maybe she'll change her mind next year and sell out…or stay and remarry."

Why did he say that? Sophy had never given him any indication she'd marry him or any man at all. Nor had he given her an indication he would ask her to.

"Sophy loaned us the use of her mule team to pull our wagon. We'll leave our oxen for you to use to bust sod. You still intend to break that patch we talked about?"

"Why would she do that?" Especially since he didn't know how to handle a team of oxen. "She didn't mention it to me."

Charles looked a little chagrined. "Well, I told her the oxen would pull the plow all day without tiring. Mules have to have breaks. I'm sure she thought she was doing you a favor."

Maybe, but it would've been nice if she'd asked him first. "I've never driven oxen."

"My team is well-trained. They'll help you keep the rows straight. All you have to do is get 'em in position and yell gee-up, then whoa at the end of the row." He laughed again. Charles had an irritating laugh.

The Huffington's left the next morning a good two hours later than they'd planned. Caleb and Sophy loitered in the yard watching the wagon as it grew too small to be distinguishable. Heidi had clung to her mother's skirts, sobbing inconsolably as she realized Susie, her playmate, had left.

Caleb dropped to his knees to get down to eye level with the little girl and dabbed her

Sophy

cheeks with his handkerchief. "They'll be back in the spring, honey, and build their own house so they can stay for good."

"When is spring?"

"After the cold and snow come and go."

"After Christmas," Sophy added.

"That's a long time." Heidi's lower lip poked out as her face primped up, ready to cry.

Caleb scooped the child up on his shoulders. "Let's go out back so you and Marty can swing."

"Where is Marty?" Sophy asked in a frantic tone, sending an alarmed gaze around the yard.

He touched her shoulder. "It's all right. I just saw him follow Sunny around the corner." After his birthday, Marty had learned to walk and now toddled all over the place, inside and out. It was amazing how fast he could go. Caleb was grateful Sunny still took her guard duty seriously.

They rounded the house and found Marty sitting in the middle of a pile of dirt Sunny had dug up and gleefully pouring handfuls over his head.

"You little scamp." Sophy took off after her baby.

Caleb followed with Heidi. He set the little girl on the ground and took stock of the yard, including the barren vegetable garden. He should plow it under so it would be ready for next year. Another chore to add to the list of everything that had to be done before winter.

There were few leaves left on the cottonwood and maple trees Sophy had transplanted a few years ago. The maples rose over his head already and were probably brought in when Sophy and Martin first claimed this land. The cottonwood trees, dug up as saplings from the woods near the river, were barely as tall as he was, but even at this height, they framed the yard, making it look like a home. So different from his own claimed land that had nothing but a three-sided soddy.

He'd decided to finish the back wall without a fireplace and turn it into a stable. His dream was to build a house of brick and mortar, but transportation costs were sky-high. If only they'd send a railroad through here. Of course, they wouldn't do that unless enough people moved in to build a town.

"Let them play in the dirt for awhile. They'll soon enough be closed up inside and you'll wish they would get outside."

Laughing, she dropped back. "That's true, and this year I'll have two to keep entertained. Last year this time Marty was still in his cradle, sleeping most of the time." Her laughter stopped and she cast a far-away look.

He knew she was thinking that last year this time Martin was still alive. Pointing to a circle of stumps, he said, "Let's take a seat while they

Sophy

play." He wanted Sophy's full attention.

The two semi-circles of stumps faced a firepit where they sometimes roasted geese, duck, or haunches of pork on a spit. Ears of corn, still in their shucks, would be laid on the hot coals and added to the meals which were eaten at a sawhorse table.

He and Sophy sat facing outward away from the pit today where they could talk and still watch the children. "Why did you loan the mules to Charles?"

Sophy seemed surprised by his question. "Why not? His oxen will cut the sod better than my mules. Martin didn't sell our oxen until all the sod was busted."

"I've never driven oxen."

She didn't answer for a while and when she did, she didn't try to hide her annoyance. "There's little difference. Martin said so."

He knew better than to dispute Martin who had used both mules and oxen and had successfully tamed this land. "Well, I guess I'll see right now. I'll take a sandwich with me so I don't have to come back for lunch."

"You don't have to do that. I'll bring it out to you." Her tone had softened. "I'd better take my rascals in and get them cleaned up." She patted him on the back and walked away.

As it turned out he didn't have as much trouble with the oxen as he'd feared. Red and

Roam were docile, considering the massive beasts they were, and they knew the sod better than Caleb. The dry weather held and it looked like he'd be able to get all the acreage of tall grass turned over to rot over the winter months.

Then two weeks after working the field, his confidence led to disaster.

He didn't know how it happened. Maybe Roam stepped into a rabbit hole. Maybe he was bit by a wasp. However it happened, the ox pulled to the right, tipping the plow over and jerking Caleb off his feet, causing him to topple on the plowshare.

Pain shot through his leg and he rolled over in the grass. Blood spewed from a gash in his thigh, halfway between his knee and hip. Judging from the flow coloring his pants leg, not to mention the pain, the gash was deep. He whipped out his belt and corded the thigh above the injury, but he knew if the cut hit a main artery, he'd bleed out here in the field before he could make it to the house.

And if he reached the house, what could Sophy do? He'd seen her doctoring Heidi's skinned knee, and she was prepared to deliver Luce's calf, but this injury might be more than a real doctor could repair. *Lord, help me.*

Whether he lived or died, he wanted Sophy, if only to tell her good-bye. He half stumbled, half crawled toward the house, sending up a prayer with each foot of ground gained. He'd never experienced this agony. The pain now

Sophy

radiated all the way down his leg and he couldn't feel his foot, growing numb from the deprivation of blood flow.

She must have been watching out the window because he was only halfway when she dashed out the door and flew across the yard. She tugged on him and he got to his feet. Her arm wrapped around his chest. "Hold onto me. Use me as a crutch."

He circled her thin shoulders and grasped the hard muscles of her arm. If it were any other woman, his weight would have crushed her. But this was a strong woman, her strength built up year after year by the work demanded of her. Still, he tried to bear as much weight on his injured leg as possible. Despite all his effort, he stumbled.

"Lean on me," she screamed.

He did and somehow, she got him into the house and laid on the sofa. Not a minute too soon as the room began to spin, and he closed his eyes against the pain.

"Ma, what's wrong with Cabub?" Heidi's small voice held a note of terror. Marty began to wail as loud as he could.

"Take Marty and Sunny and go to your room. Stay there until I get you," Sophy ordered.

"Ma, Cabub is hurt."

Sophy must have taken the children to their room because he heard a door closing and

Marty's cries faded. She returned with a basket containing bottles and bags and a book entitled *Simples Medicine*. All except the book, tucked under her arm, was in a pan secured in the crook of one arm, while she carried a steaming kettle in her hand. A pile of rags and cloths were draped over her shoulder.

Caleb closed his eyes against the pain. He was in good hands. Sophy was the next best thing to a doctor. He relaxed as she took his boot and sock off. He didn't have to look to know his foot was purple. He'd already lost feeling.

"I'm going to have to cut your pants leg off." Her voice sounded very close to his ear. "The tourniquet has to be removed immediately."

He nodded, but already felt the blade of her scissors as she cut the pants up to wound area. "Is it still bleeding?" he asked.

"Yes, but not badly, but we won't know if an artery was hit until the tourniquet is removed." She pressed a thick pad of cotton fabric to the wound. Taking his hand, she moved it to cover the pad. "Do you think you can press down on this cloth while I loosen the belt?"

He craned his neck, trying to get a good look. "You do that. I'll release the belt."

"All right, but go slow. Let it slip through the buckle a little bit at the time."

He already knew to do that, but he just nodded his agreement. Finding the end of the leather belt and the buckle, he did as she'd asked.

"Whoa." Her sharp command froze his hand. "Hold it there while I wash the wound."

He wished he could see the gash. The bleeding had increased. He could both feel and see the blood everywhere. "It's going to ruin your sofa."

"I keep the oil cloth on it while the children play in the house. It was in place."

He hadn't noticed when he laid down, but he couldn't notice anything but the pain and the burden he'd placed on Sophy. But he should have known she'd be prepared for everything.

The splash of water told him she was preparing to wash the wound. Then the soapy water jolted him. He couldn't keep from jerking and loosing the belt a bit more. She grabbed his hand that held the belt. "Steady. You can't let it go until I've stitched the wound."

He gritted his teeth against the pain and asked, "You're going to do that?"

"I'll have to in order to stop the bleeding. I'm thinking it didn't cut into a main vein or artery, so stitching it up and cloth compresses should stop the flow." She didn't have to add that if she couldn't stop the bleeding he wouldn't survive.

Oddly enough, he wasn't afraid. That peace without understanding had covered him like a warm blanket and he trusted the outcome.

Whether he trusted God or Sophy more, he didn't know. It didn't matter. They were working in unison.

The smell of whiskey pervaded the air, surprising him. He'd never seen her take a drink, and he doubted Martin had been a drinking man. She must keep it for medicinal purposes. Maybe she expected him to drink it to dull the pain.

Instead of offering it to him, she poured it on his wound, and burning seared his whole leg. He couldn't prevent a yell and would've released the belt if her hand wasn't again holding his.

"I'm sorry, I know it burns fierce, but I had to wash the wound out with whiskey to prevent infection. If it festers up, you could lose your leg. I've seen it before."

Although he wanted to cry, he laughed instead as an image of Sophy sawing off his leg flashed before him. He had no doubt she'd do it to save his life.

She ignored his hysterics and pushed his hand away from the tourniquet. He felt it tightening as she grunted with the effort. "I have to get the bleeding to stop so I can see how to stitch the gash," she said.

Apparently satisfied with the way things were going, Sophy stood and searched through her basket of medicines. She took a bottle out of the basket and poured the liquid in a spoon. "What's that?" he asked.

Sophy

"Laudanum. It'll relieve the pain when I push a needle through your skin." She touched his mouth with the spoon and he swallowed the nasty stuff. "It should take effect by the time I get the needle and thread ready."

"Where did you learn all this?"

"I helped the nurse who treated children at the orphanage where I stayed. I was fascinated and watched her carefully. I even dreamed of becoming a nurse."

"Then you met Martin and gave up your dream."

"Then I came to love Martin and my dreams were realized." The softness that had crept into her voice changed to that take-charge tone she normally used as she said, "There, I've finished the stitching and the bleeding has stopped." She bandaged the wound and released the belt.

He flinched as the blood began to flow.

"Do you want that other teaspoon of laudanum?"

"No, I'll be all right. The stuff makes me sleepy."

"Good, you need sleep." She smiled as she began gathering her doctoring items. "I'd better go bring my children in here to see you've been patched up."

She'd leaned over him, reaching for the soiled rags. A tendril fell over her face and he reached to tuck it back behind her ear. Their gazes met in a new look that caught them both unaware. The room fell away as they searched each other, reaching into the other's soul.

Amazingly, tears came into her eyes and hovered on her lashes.

"Thank you, Sophy."

She inclined her head. "We'll pray you recover without infection."

Before he could understand what had happened between them, she was gone.

Chapter 12

Caleb's wound didn't get infected and the stubborn man went back to work much sooner than Sophy thought he should. Not that she didn't need his help as the first snowflakes fell soon after his accident.

One thing she rejoiced over even as the hours of daylight grew shorter was sitting in the parlor with Caleb and the children before a blazing fire. Her hands kept busy knitting, mending, sewing. There was plenty of that. They all needed warm stockings for the great cold wind that blew stronger every day.

She could no longer pretend her feelings for Caleb were changing as she saw him not as a brother or a friend, but as a man. Guilt gnawed at her insides for allowing another take Martin's place in her heart so soon. How could that happen when she'd loved Martin with all she had?

There was nothing wrong with that, the logical side of her mind told her. She and Caleb had been brought together by circumstances neither had foreseen or wanted. And as Alma had reminded her often enough, women—and men, too—didn't have the luxury to delay a remarriage out here on the harsh prairie.

Not that Caleb had given her any indication he saw her as anything more than a friend. She was just someone to lean on because no one else was available yet, and he was waiting to go home to meet his intended. He would have already left if not for her. Only his promise to Martin and God to help her through the winter kept him here.

No one knew better than she just how harsh the weather could be. How could she have taken care of the stock and all the unexpected things that could, and no doubt would, happen? How could she have cut enough wood to keep the house warm without Caleb? It now stacked up to the ceiling of the back porch.

Even as she gazed at the darkening skies that December morning, snowflakes fluttered across the window almost sideways. It had been sleeting earlier, but the wind and skies told her a blizzard was coming.

"It's snowing, Ma."

Heidi startled Sophy. "Yes, looks like we're in for a lot of it this time." They had had a few snow storms earlier, but they'd only amounted to a few inches that had all melted except for the

Sophy

shady patches. If she could read the weather right, and she knew she could, this blizzard would leave a couple of feet, possibly more, and they wouldn't see the ground again until the spring thaw.

"Let us go out and play in it, Ma. Sunny will watch us."

Sophy wanted to refuse. It would take time she didn't have to bundle the children up. She had to finish the wash before the snow put out the fire under her washpot. But this might be their last chance for days to get outside. She didn't look forward to the time when they would get cranky from boredom and she would have to wash diapers in the kitchen, then hanging them on the porch to freeze dry. If she could just get this wash on the line this stiff wind would dry them in less than an hour.

She didn't leave the children outside long. It was just too cold and the snow was coming down harder. Every few minutes she watched for Caleb. Surely he wasn't still out there in the field. At breakfast he'd said he intended to continue breaking his horses to the plow before the ground froze, and had taken a sandwich with him so he didn't have to come in for lunch.

Still, she worried. What if he'd had another accident? He could be lying out there, snow covering him, unable to move. She'd convinced herself to go look for him when he blew through the front door on a gust of wind and a swirl of white flakes.

He sat on the bench beside the door and began taking off his boots. "Sorry to get the floor wet, but since I'll have to use your washroom to wash up, I didn't bother to go around back."

"I'll mop it up. Supper is on the table when you're ready," Sophy said. The idea he felt the need to explain himself to her after months of practically living with them bothered her. She wished he'd consider himself part of the family.

Heidi stopped before Caleb and patted his cheek. "It's all right, Cabub. My boots got the floor wet, too."

"You saying I'm as messy as you, little bit—and you, littler bit." Caleb tickled first Heidi and then Marty under the chin. Both children shrieked and fell into giggles. Caleb scooped them up, one under each arm, and carried them to the kitchen.

Heidi and Marty certainly thought Caleb was part of the family. What would happen to them when he moved into his own house—with his wife?

What would happen to her?

After supper, Caleb brought a book into the parlor where she and the children waited for him. Sophy kept her hands busy with knitting or sewing, but truth to tell, she looked forward to this time as much as the children did. It really wouldn't have mattered what he read, as long as she could hear the cadence of his voice.

"I found a new book I think you'll really

like, Heidi. Look it has your name on it," he said.

Sophy's daughter drew in an exaggerated breath. "Oooh, I have a book about me? Where did you find it, Cabub?"

"I found it in the books my mother packed for me." He glanced over Heidi's head to find Sophy's eyes. "Don't know why she sent me a children's book." He laughed. "Probably still thinks of me as a child."

"Or maybe it's a hint that she wants grandchildren one day."

"She has five grandchildren from my older brothers."

"But not from you." The look that passed between them was one she couldn't quite decipher, though she'd seen it several times before. The color in his eyes deepened, or maybe that was a trick of the light. She shouldn't read more into his looks than was there.

After what seemed to be a long time, he pulled his gaze from hers. "It's not about you, Heidi, but about a little girl with the same name that went to live with her grandfather in the mountains of a faraway country." He shifted Marty, who sat on his lap.

Everyone rushed through supper, offering little conversation. The wind beat against the shutters, keeping Sophy's nerves on edge but quieting the children who startled each time something hit the house, too frightened to make a sound of their own. She had to remain calm for their sake.

For his part, Caleb seemed deep in thought. Did he regret not leaving with the Huffingtons? Was he imagining what he was missing at his family's home, where there was light and laughter? Where he wouldn't have to get out and face the wind and snow? Instead, he'd have to huddle under buffalo hides on a cold, hard bed tonight just so he could give her a sense of propriety.

The shrieking wind didn't seem as loud in the parlor. Sophy sat in her rocker on one side of the fireplace, while Caleb sat opposite on the sofa with the children. The drone of his voice soothed her nerves as her fingers worked the piece of knitting without any conscious thought.

When she returned to the parlor after getting the children to bed, she found Caleb bundled up and at the door. The shutters still rattled like they'd come off their hinges at any moment and the wind created a down draft in the chimney, making the flames in the fireplace dance.

"I doubt you can get out the front door," she said. "Likely the snow is blocking it. You can go through the back." She tried to read his thoughts behind his brooding eyes. "If you insist on going out in this storm."

Caleb made his way toward the kitchen and she followed him, unable to let him leave, she said, "How about a cup of coffee before you go?"

Sophy

He turned and gave her a smile that set those familiar butterflies fluttering in her stomach. "I'd like that. Maybe it would keep me warm until I reach the barn."

She doubted that as she grabbed the pot and filled it with water. Coffee beans had already been ground for breakfast. "It's too dark in here." She'd already turned down the lamp, trying to save her oil and kerosene. It had to last through the winter.

Caleb turned up the lamp before she got to it. The light failed to lift her spirits much, but it helped. Of all the things she hated about the dead of winter, it was the lack of light.

She got out two mugs and poured for Caleb and then herself. "I don't have any cream. The children drank all the milk today."

"That's all right. Wish that cow of yours would have her calf soon. Lou is drying up fast."

Sophy sat in the chair adjacent to his. "I'd have thought Luce would already have had her calf. I've never understood why animals choose the coldest weather to give birth."

Caleb laughed. "It just seems that way, I guess, but Luce can't last long."

They sipped their coffee in silence, the wind still whipping the shutters and screaming at the eaves.

Caleb set his empty mug down with a thud. Sophy sprang to her feet. "Can I get you a refill?"

He waved his palm in her direction. "No thanks. I'd better go so you can go to bed."

"I can't, not tonight." No, she wouldn't be able to sleep this night. She knew these blizzards. In years past, both cold and fear would set her trembling until Martin took her in his arms and held her tight—all night long.

"Why not?"

Against her will, tears rose in her eyes, blinding her. She looked around wildly for a napkin to wipe them. Caleb moved around the chairs and laid his hand on her shoulder. "It's all right, Sophy, It sounds worse than it is. I think it'll blow out by morning."

She raised her face to him. His features looked distorted through the film of her tears. "I'm so tired of being alone. I'm afraid of winter storms, have been since I was caught out in one and nearly froze."

He rubbed circles on her back, meant to comfort though they brought fresh tears. Because he'd soon be gone and she would be all alone. Afraid of the night.

"Your house is safe and warm. You'll be fine. The children are sleeping peacefully, even through the noise."

"I know. It's just me. Martin used to hold me all night by the fire." A strangled laugh escaped her lips. "He would fall asleep, but every time something crashed against the house, I awoke." She drew in a lungful of air.

Sophy

"Then I'd realize he held me and I felt safe."

Her gaze met Caleb's troubled eyes. "But Martin is gone and I have no one to hold me." She sobbed. His arms came around her, and she rested her head on his shoulder as he eased her back to the sofa.

It wasn't proper for him to sleep in the same house with her, even if no one would know but them. She should be ashamed of tempting him. She should let him go now. Caleb wanted to watch the cow—the other stock. But when he sat beside her and hugged her to him, she couldn't have stopped him any more than she could stop the howling wind.

He rocked her as he would Heidi and rubbed circles on her back. The sound of his racing heart as she rested her ear against his chest gave her the only evidence he was as affected by their embrace as she was.

She tilted her head up to find his eyes. "I'm sorry I'm so weak," she croaked.

He shifted her in his arm and caressed her cheek. "Nothing about you is weak, Sophy. You're the strongest woman I've ever seen, and you have a tender heart. Aside from that you're...beautiful."

She could easily have moved out of his arms even as he lowered his mouth to hers, but it would have taken Charles's oxen team to have pulled them apart. She needed his kiss. Everything in her fiber wanted it.

And it was everything she thought it would be—gentle, probing—with a yearning that matched hers. It was as if all the passion they'd locked up tight burst through at once, overwhelming her. She didn't want it to end and if it had been up to her, it wouldn't have, but with a moan, he broke the connection and pressed her face to his shoulder, holding her firmly in place as if he feared they would continue the kiss until neither could stop.

She felt his touch as he stroked her hair, a tender touch that soothed her, taking her away from the storm.

He held her there until she fell asleep in his arms.

In the morning he was gone, along with the shrieking wind.

They never spoke of the passion they'd shared that night, and he slept in the barn except during the blizzards that came. There were but three of them that winter, and each time he took her to the sofa and held her until she slept.

His touch was just as comforting, but he never kissed her again.

As the light of day dimmed during December, both Sophy and Caleb grabbed every bit of the sunlight they could, rushing to finish those chores that had to be done before snow and ice would coat the land.

One morning Caleb surprised her by

Sophy

coming in from outside with a scrubby pine tree. "What is that for?"

"This is Christmas Eve. Didn't you know that? Are the kids up yet?"

It couldn't be, but the calendar confirmed it. She rushed to fetch a blanket to wrap around the pail holding the tree. It sure was puny compared to the trees Martin would bring in. Martin remembered the German motherland and the great Christmas celebrations of his village. She'd have to pop some popcorn for stringing. Heidi was old enough this year to help.

She already had the children's presents stored away and apples, oranges, and walnuts they'd all enjoy.

The next morning, the little stockings were hung and the presents resting under the tree when Heidi and Marty run into the room, their eyes big, their smiles wide. After the opening of presents and a Christmas breakfast, Caleb said. "Let's play a game with the walnuts."

Heidi and Marty had been tossing them for Sunny to fetch. "What kind of game, Cabub?" Heidi asked.

"It's kind of like hide and seek. You and Marty go hide and when I call you, you have to find the walnuts I've hidden. The one who finds the most walnuts gets a special treat."

"We'll hide in our room," Heidi said. "Come with us, Sunny." The children and dog ran down the hall, Marty bringing up the rear.

Sophy laughed as Caleb went around the room hiding the walnuts under blankets, pillows behind the stack of wood. "Did you just make up that game?"

"Yes, but I was afraid they were going to break something throwing them for Sunny to fetch. This way is safer."

"In spite of everything, this has been a good Christmas," she said.

Caleb straightened from the place he'd crouched. His gaze scanned the room before landing on her. "It has for a fact. We've been blessed. It just proves that everywhere we're gathered together in His name, there is joy...and love.

When the Huffingtons returned in the spring, Caleb mounted his big stallion and left to return to his family.

Chapter 13

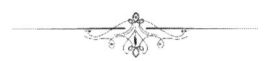

The Beckman's Farm near Harrisburg, Illinois

Caleb woke before daylight. As his eyes adjusted to the dim light, he wondered where he was. Certainly not in Sophy's barn, but the dream had been so vivid, it took him a couple of minutes to realize he was in his old bedroom in his parents' big farmhouse. Had been for the past week.

He threw off the covers, not surprised at the dream since his mind had been filled with that farm on the Dakota prairie every minute of the day and night since he'd been visiting Ma and Pa. If it wasn't thoughts of Sophy, it was the children. How they'd grown. How Heidi had cried when he left. He'd even dreamed about the cows and horses. The cow had dropped twin heifers after that first blizzard and he wondered if Sophy had decided to keep one and put Luce out to pasture.

Luce was getting too old to bear another calf. Farmers usually slaughtered a cow that got too old. But Sophy was so tender-hearted. She said Luce had dropped three calves since she'd had the cow and provided the family with milk through the years. Luce had deserved to enjoy the rest of her days grazing in the pasture.

He thought of all these things lying there in the dark. Almost all of his waking hours were filled with thoughts of Sophy.

He had enjoyed seeing his family again. His two older brothers and their wives had visited, as had his sister, her husband and children. They were all farmers now, including David, the preacher, and couldn't stay long. Caleb could ill afford to stay away from his land, either. Today, his folks would have to understand.

The approaching dawn dragged its light slowly. Pa would already be out at the barn and Caleb should be helping him like he'd been doing every day since he'd been home. But he wanted to talk to his ma today. Had to before he left.

He got up and dressed. Pulling the drapes back from his bedroom's one window, he realized it was as he suspected. A cloudy day. A good reason to start out for home today. Trains weren't impeded by the rain.

Funny that he didn't see his folks' house as

Sophy

home anymore, which was all the more strange, because he hadn't built his own house on his homesite. There was only one explanation. Somewhere in the deeper reaches of his mind, he considered Sophy's house home. He thought of her and her children as his family.

And he would return with the hope of making them just that—his family.

A clatter of pans told him his mother was up. She might not have to do as much now that it was just her and Pa, but the farm woman in her made her get up at first light.

He clumped his boots on the floor while making his way to the kitchen so as not to startle her. She wasn't used to him being in the house, and he'd already scared her twice by coming up on her unawares.

"Can I help?" He let his words precede him.

She was stooped over the low cabinet of her pantry, retrieving an iron skillet. A smile created double laugh lines in her still young-looking face, though her chestnut colored hair was shot with silver. "Good morning, son. Yes, you can fetch the milk pail from the back porch. I heard your pa set it down out there a few minutes ago."

He pulled her to her feet and kissed her cheek. "I'll be right back. Collecting milk and eggs was always my chore from the time I was five, if I remember correctly." Pa had insisted Caleb spend his time visiting, not taking care of the farm. But Caleb missed the everyday chores back in Dakota—the smell of the barn, greeting the horses and cows and hens.

Setting the pail, full of frothy milk, on his mother's spacious counter, he tried to gather the nerve to tell her he was leaving today.

"Would you prefer pancakes or biscuits today?" she asked, her back to him, standing before the stove.

"How about both?"

She chuckled. "All right, why not?"

"You've certainly fed me well the past week. You must be worn out cooking for all of us."

"Oh, posh, you know how I enjoy cooking."

"Well, it was all delicious, and if I didn't have Spike to exercise every morning, I'd have grown fat."

Ma laughed out loud. "Fat? You? I'm sure you eat just as hearty on your homestead. You told me Sophy's biscuits were as good as mine."

He had? That was a stupid thing to do. His pa had always admonished him, "You never should compare someone else's cooking to your mother's." But in truth, Sophy's cooking was as good, including her biscuits, not so much as the taste, but the little things she did with them. She didn't bother with cutting them out, but rolled them in her palm and pressed her knuckles in each biscuit before baking. She always pinched off smaller biscuits for the children.

Sophy

"I'm glad you've enjoyed the food, at least," Ma pulled him out of his musings.

"I've enjoyed everything about my visit, Ma, but there's so much work to be done back in Dakota, I better head out after breakfast."

"Your Pa and I will miss you a powerful lot, but I'm not surprised you're anxious to get back. You kept looking out the window when Clarise was here." She set the mugs and coffee pot on the table. "Want to tell me about it?"

He strode to the china cabinet. "I wasn't a very attentive host to Clarise. I'm sorry." He set the table and sat in the chair he normally took.

Ma dished up a plate of scrambled eggs. "That's all right, honey, it's hard to be attentive when your heart is far away."

He wasn't surprised Ma could see through him. She'd always been able to do that. "Clarise released me. She's in love with some other fellow."

"She told you that when she visited us last week? You don't seem upset by it."

He didn't bother to answer. "I have to settle things with Sophy."

His mother set a plate of hot biscuits in the middle of the table. She didn't look the least bit surprised. "I'm glad you came. I wanted to see you and I wanted you to settle things with Clarise. I'd promised her mother, you see." She took her chair and reached out to take his hand for the blessing.

After their amens, she said, "I'm glad you came mainly so I could see for myself where your affection lay." She jumped back up to gather the jam and butter.

"Just promise me one thing," she said.

"What's that?"

"You'll bring your Sophy here to get married."

He bit the side of his lip. "That's the trouble, Ma. I don't know if she'll marry me. There are complications."

She sat back down and poured the coffee. "With matters of the heart, there are always complications."

"See, the thing is, she depends on me, leans on me, but I don't know whether she loves me, or just needs me. You know what I'm saying?"

"Yes, but need may only be the first layer of a woman's feelings. I need your father. It's one of the reasons I love him."

Caleb poured cream in his coffee and stirred absently. He appreciated his mother's advice. He'd have sought her advice earlier but had thought she was set on him marrying Clarise. "But sometimes I get the impression she sees me as a replacement for Martin, her dead husband, and she may always see me that way."

"That she can't love you for yourself, is that

Sophy

it?"

"Yes." He shook his head. "Maybe I'm asking too much."

"You are not asking too much. No man should marry a woman unless she loves him more than anyone except God." Ma took two of the crispy strips of bacon to her eggs and biscuit, giving him a pointed look. "Have you prayed about this?"

"You know I have, constantly."

"Well, that's your answer, sweetheart. When you feel God's peace about your decision, propose to this widow." Ma salted her scrambled eggs like what she'd just said was the easiest thing in the world to do.

"And I have only one request," she added, "that you bring her to meet us and have your wedding in our church." She buttered her biscuit and gave him a wink. "I'll watch those delightful children while you and Sophy go on a well-deserved honeymoon."

"Honeymoon? Ma, I think you're getting a little ahead of yourself."

"No, you just need to speed up, son," Ma said, as Pa entered the room. "Don't you think so, dear?"

Pa took his place at the table. "Absolutely."

"You don't even know what we're talking about." Caleb couldn't help but smile at the prospect Ma had painted. As for Pa, he hadn't even mentioned Sophy to him.

Pa surprised him by saying, "Your prospective marriage to Sophy. What else could it be? I told your mother her little scheme to have it out with Clarise was unnecessary. Of the four pages of those letters you sent us since meeting the lady farmer, at least three were about Sophy."

"Was I that obvious?"

Pa just chuckled as he filled his plate. "I was dawdling out in the barn so your ma could talk with you. I knew she could set you straight. That's one of the reasons you need a good woman—to keep you straight.

Chapter 14

Back on the North Dakota Farm

"Would you believe your peas have already sprouted?" Alma asked.

Sophy heard her but she was staring so intently to the southeast, she didn't answer. Staring wouldn't bring him back any sooner, but it made her feel better.

"Charles says the corn is already up, too. What about your wheat?"

Sophy was proud of her wheat crop. She'd planted the field Caleb had left furrowed herself. "It shot up like always."

"And like always, the weeds will sprout." Alma stretched. "Martin sure does miss Caleb. It takes at least two men to keep ahead. When did you say he'd be back?"

Alma knew when Caleb planned to return. "In three days," Sophy answered without thinking. "Maybe earlier."

The other woman laughed. "Well, he surely hasn't had time to court a woman and marry. I think you ought to let him know how you feel."

"He knows how I feel."

"Have you told him how you feel about him?"

Sophy released the breath she'd been holding. "He hasn't said how he feels about me." Everyone knew the man had the prerogative in such things. A woman had to wait.

And pray. Sophy had been able to leave Caleb in God's hands every night as she prayed. Caleb had said they were brought together by circumstances, but surly God guided their circumstances.

Didn't God put Caleb in Martin's path before the accident, and thereby brought him and Sophy together? She had to believe that. But each night, she asked God to do what was best for Caleb. He deserved only the best. And God would give her the peace to accept whatever happened.

It was a woman's place to wait, but the waiting was hard.

"Ma...Ma." Heidi's call pulled Sophy's attention from the garden to her daughter, who was running as fast as her little legs could pump.

Sophy

Marty toddled up from the hole he'd been trying to dig.

Heidi skidded to a stop. "Ma, it's Cabub. He's coming, Ma." When Sophy didn't immediately react, the little girl grabbed her hand. "Come see, Ma."

Sophy used her hand to shade her eyes from the mid-morning sun. "I can see a buggy, Heidi, but that doesn't mean it's Caleb. It's likely someone passing through." No, that's not what it meant. He'd brought a buggy back with him, which could only mean one thing—Clarise was with him. He could've ridden his horse back if he was alone. Her heart fell like a rock into her stomach.

Lord, give me peace.

"No matter who it is," Alma said, "I'd better get the coffee on." Every passer-by who stopped would expect some refreshment, and every settler was always ready with hot coffee.

"It is Cabub, Ma," Heidi insisted.

Sophy squinted. The horse looked Caleb's and she couldn't see anyone sitting beside him. Maybe her eyes were seeing only what she wanted to see. Marty pulled on her skirt, and without looking at him, she absent-mindedly scooped him up to rest on her hip. It did look like Caleb.

The man on the buggy waved. It was Caleb. Sophy gathered her skirt in her free hand and ran, Heidi with her. Her brain told her it was foolish to run out to meet the buggy. In a few minutes he'd be here. Her heart told her if she could cut off a few seconds by meeting him, she'd do it.

Her feet flew through the short grass. She blessed the men for harvesting the hay last fall, so the new growth didn't impede her as the virgin prairie would. Marty bounced on her hip, straining her strength, but that didn't slow her as she moved ahead of little Heidi.

It was fitting the children were with her. In Sophy's mind, they all belonged together.

When they were about fifty yards apart, Caleb jumped from the buggy and met them halfway. More like collided into each other's arms. "We missed you so much." That sounded silly. He'd only been gone a little over two weeks. She ought to pull herself together.

But Caleb held her tight, squashing Marty between them until he squealed, and Sunny jumped up on all of them in her excitement to have Caleb home.

When Sophy stepped back to give the child some air, Caleb tossed him up in the air, then set him on the ground. He patted Sunny's head, then scooped Heidi up and tossed her.

When he would have put Heidi down, she grabbed him around the neck. "We're so glad you're home. We need you."

He kissed Heidi's forehead and let her slide to the ground. "It's good to be needed." His gaze

Sophy

drifted from the children to Sophy. "I enjoyed visiting my folks, but they don't need me."

Questions swirled around Sophy, but she was afraid to voice them. After they'd stared into each other's eyes longer than necessary, she asked, "You didn't make plans with Clarise?"

He smiled and she noticed he was clean shaven, his smile lines stretching wide. "We made plans—she for herself and me for myself. Clarise decided she didn't want to make her home far away from everything she knew, and she met someone who could give her a home in St. Louis. That was a relief to me because, dear Sophy, when I compared Clarise to you…she didn't measure up."

"She didn't?" Her voice had fallen to a whisper. How he could hear her above the ever-present wind she didn't know. But he did.

"No. I enjoyed visiting with my folks, but I'm glad to be home. I realized, you see, my home is wherever you are."

"You're not disappointed about Clarise?" Surely, he must have felt something about her rejection.

"Forget Clarise. She found another easily enough, and she had sense enough to realize I wasn't the one for her." He turned serious eyes on Sophy. "All the way home I've been praying you'll see I love no one but you, and you might love me enough to marry me."

Her heart leaped into her throat, choking

off what she wanted to say. Instead tears spilled down her cheeks and she gripped his hand like it was a lifeline.

"I intended to come back early and court you, but that isn't necessary, is it? I already know your heart and you already know mine. Maybe you knew better than I did. I was so afraid I wouldn't give you enough time to grieve. I didn't want you to look upon me as a replacement for Martin, but that you'd love me for myself."

As she hadn't wanted to be a replacement for Clarise. His eyes said she wasn't and she let her tears wash away any doubt about his love.

He coughed into his elbow then pierced her with another soul-deep gaze. "Do you, Sophy? Do you love just me?"

Somehow she found her voice. "I do, Caleb, I've loved you for months, but I didn't know how much until this past winter."

He shifted his glance to the children, standing silent, holding each other's hand, staring with big, blue eyes, their mouths hanging open. "I can't wait another minute to claim you, Sophy. To claim our children." He dropped to one knee. "Will you marry me?"

Did he even have to ask? She wondered what the Huffingtons must think as they were all out in the yard, looking their way. She didn't care. Besides, they'd be pleased, but what about Caleb's family?

Sophy

"Yes, yes. I love you with my whole heart, Caleb, only you. Will your family approve?"

He rose and pulled her into a close hug. "They know my intentions, yes. Ma wants us to come and get married in our church in Harrisburg. She promises to take care of the children so we can spend a honeymoon in New Orleans. It's nice in the spring."

A honeymoon? She'd never been on a honeymoon nor visited so far just for the enjoyment. "When?" A million thoughts swirled through her mind. There was so much to do on the farm. But Caleb relieved her of those worries.

"Right away." He chuckled. "Ma is already making preparations. The Huffingtons will take care of the crops and the stock while we're gone. We'll make it up to them by helping them build their house. I had already discussed that possibility with Charles before I left."

She couldn't keep the smile off her face. "God has answered all my prayers...well, all I really asked for was that you'd come back to me."

Caleb swung Heidi up on his shoulders and tucked Marty under his left arm. He offered Sophy his right, and she hugged herself to him. They walked back to the buggy and with all of them seated, he leaned over and kissed her cheek. "How do you like this rig, my love, it's my family's wedding present to us."

"I like it just fine, dear future husband of mine," she said, sinking in the comfortable leather seat. It didn't really matter to her. Anywhere beside him would be just fine. With the children and Sunny tucked into the back seat, they made their way home.

Chapter 15

Time passed in a joyous blur for Sophy. After packing two trunks, one for her, one for the children, they bid the Huffingtons good-bye and took the riverboat to Grand Forks. From there they traveled by train to Harrisburg.

Caleb's large, boisterous family overwhelmed her at first. There were so many and all vying for her attention. Besides, the men called Caleb from her side for one purpose or another. But then, the women—Mrs. Beckham and her daughter and daughters-in-law—kept her so busy readying for the wedding, she couldn't miss Caleb's attention much.

The wedding itself was set for the Sunday after they'd arrived, and Sophy expected it to be a simple affair. So, when Mrs. Beckham—Jenny she'd insisted Sophy call her—took her to a dress shop to pick up her wedding dress, she'd gasped.

The dress she'd worn at her first wedding was a blue and white calico which had since been worn out and turned into scraps. As she gazed upon this dress, she couldn't believe such a beautiful concoction could have been created in such a short length of time.

The folds of pale lavender silk shimmered with every move. The bodice, overlaid with lace and seed pearls fit her beautifully, although the dressmaker assured her she'd have it altered to perfection before Saturday. "I could easily have worn my one Sunday dress," she told Jenny as they left the shop. I don't believe Caleb would care."

Jenny laughed. "I agree. Caleb wouldn't care if you were wearing a feed sack." Her future mother-in-law gave her a side hug. "But you deserve this day, Sophy, so you'll remember it forever, and pass it on to Heidi maybe as an evening gown if she should prefer pure white for her wedding."

"I'll have time to think about that. Thank you for doing all this for me and for taking care of Heidi and Marty while...," she couldn't help blushing. "While Caleb and I are gone."

"Oh, my dear, I enjoy it. I had only the one daughter to organize a grand wedding for. It's I who thank you for giving me another chance. Besides, both Tom and I enjoy the children."

"And they enjoy you. In fact, Heidi told me last night she now had a grandfather like the one in the book. I'm afraid she expects him to take

Sophy

her to the mountains."

Jenny laughed. "And he'll take her and all of you out west to see where he grew up. Oh, yes, I overheard Tom and Heidi laying their plans."

"I was afraid…afraid you might not think me good enough for your son."

"I might have at first, but when I met you—no, even before that—when Caleb came home and I saw the love he had for you. Well, I knew I'd love you, too." Jenny gave Sophy a side hug. "And so I do."

Tears gathered in Sophy's eyes. "It means so much to me. I've never had a family other than my husband and children. I do hope you and Mr. Beckham will come to visit our farm."

"We've discussed it and we both would like to come for a few days during harvest."

Sophy and Caleb had little time for each other during that week, but Sunday, when they all gathered in the small country church and exchanged their vows, surrounded by his large family and friends, Sophy knew they would never be apart for as long as they lived together.

And she prayed that would be a great number of years.

Epilogue

One Year Later

Activity on the Beckham-Schneider farm reached a state of constant motion. Caleb and Sophy had labored constantly on their new house since last thaw, frantic to get it livable before Caleb's parents arrived. She should be thinking of Jenny and Tom as her parents, too, but that still felt strange. She'd resolved to call them Ma and Pa during their long visit here. Then, in April Sophy left the farm and construction work to give birth to James Edward—Jimmy, as Heidi dubbed him.

    Sophy swaddled the baby after his mid-afternoon nursing and made her way to her new front porch. Caleb had insisted on building it as soon as their lumber came off the boat last fall. The wide porch had its own roof and,

Sophy

according to Caleb, the whole structure could be easily moved to their new house, going up on the land Caleb had claimed that first year.

Since Sophy and Caleb were married, the Land Office had allowed them to join their claims as one and it was proved up last fall. They now owned two hundred and forty acres, one hundred and sixty acres reserved for wheat and corn growing. Their ranch house and horse farm would take up the rest of the acreage.

Charles and Alma Huffington were still preparing the sod for their farm, but their large wood and brick home would be finished before winter. And a new family had claimed the land on the other side of the Huffingtons. They were a real farming community now, and before long could incorporate a township.

She nudged the rocker with her toe and let her gaze rove the land. God had blessed her and Caleb mightily. She still had questions about why God would take Martin so young. That must be one of those things she wouldn't understand until she reached Heaven herself.

But then, it wouldn't make any difference. Time wouldn't matter. There would be no difference from the beginning to the end. Of anything. All she could do was make the most of the blessings God had sent her way now, and let her faith carry her though the hard times to come.

She let her head fall back against the chair's back, her focus on the baby's sweet, sleeping face. The hard times would be made easier if she remembered these golden days when her children where small. When the love between her and her husband was new.

A rustling sound brought her gaze up to find Alma coming. She stopped the chair from rocking. "Can I get you and the others some cold lemonade?" That was about the only effort her overly careful husband would allow her after the baby was born. That was five weeks ago and she'd recovered from childbirth, but careful husband insisted she wait the customary six weeks. Why, Papa told her after Sophy's birth, Mama had gotten out of bed and returned to the fields, Sophy tied to her chest with a flour sack.

Of course, Papa was known to exaggerate at times.

Alma swished her palm as she climbed the steps. "No, don't get up. I just came to tell you the news. I'll take a pitcher of lemonade back with me in a few minutes." She leaned over as she spoke and ran a finger along Jimmy's face.

"What news? Pull up that other rocker so we can talk low so we don't wake Jimmy. He was up half the night with colic."

Alma poked out her lower lip. "Poor little thing. I remember colic with Lenny." She tsked as she dragged the rocker closer. "You know my Jane married Pastor Jackson's son back in Missouri?"

Sophy

Yes, Sophy was happy for Jane, though she still thought the girl was too young to get married. "You've heard from Jane?"

"Oh, yes, a long letter. I could read the happiness though the lines. It does this mother's heart good, as you'll understand when your Heidi gets married."

Sophy chuckled under her breath. "Well, I have a few years yet. What is Jane's news."

"An answer to what we've been praying about. I got her letter yesterday, you know, when Mr. Rand brought our mail. I didn't want to say anything to you until I'd mentioned it to the men. Something like this has to have their approval...but, guess what? They think it's a fine idea."

If Alma was a man, she might have been a playwright. She loved to build up drama. "I'm busting to know what the news is, Alma." Sophy let her voice rise and little Jimmy jerked his arms up. She set the rocker going again. "You going to tell me or do I have to wait until Caleb comes in?"

"I should wait and let him tell you, but you know me. I can't set on a secret." Alma laughed and sent a furtive glance toward the construction site where the men worked on Sophy's and Caleb's new house. "A circuit preacher Pastor Jackson knows came visiting, bringing his new wife with him—a school teacher. They got married somewhere out west, but the teacher had to give up her school because, you know, they don't allow married women to teach."

She paused long enough for Sophy to ask, "What does that have to do with us? Is this circuit preacher looking for a home church." It would be hard to take a wife with him on his circuit of churches."

Alma nodded. "Yes, Jane told them all about our little community is growing with the Comings family claiming the land north of us, and how we were praying for a church.

"And this preacher and his teacher wife are going to settle here?"

"They were mighty excited to hear about the land and are coming out next month to look it over." Alma reached over to pat Sophy's knee. "Caleb had a wonderful idea just now. He said they could stay in this house when you all move out, and when the Wenhams—that's their name—build their place, the house can be a church and school."

Sophy smiled. "That would be wonderful. Caleb and I were wondering what we'd do with this place. It is a nice house even if half of it is soddy."

"Oh, oh, I see Caleb coming. Don't you tell him I spilled the beans, now, act surprised."

Alma got up and put her rocker back in place. "I'd better get back out there and make sure those young'uns don't get in the way." She let slip a giggle. "Sunny's having a hard time

Sophy

keeping them all corralled, what with my three little ones and the two belonging to the Commings."

Sophy got up and took Jimmy to his cradle in the bedroom where it would be quiet. She left the door open so she could hear him if he awoke and trekked to the kitchen to fix a tall glass of lemonade for Caleb. She'd just finished stirring in the sugar when the front door opened.

Caleb came up behind her. When he leaned in and nuzzled her neck, she shivered and the familiar coils of delight wrapped around her middle. She turned in his arms and reached up to kiss him, though she had to stand on tiptoe. As he held her, moving in to deepen the kiss, the floor fell away. They broke the kiss and their gazes locked. She soaked up the love in his eyes as easily as a sponge absorbed water.

Coming back down to earth, she noticed they were in front of the window, in full view of everyone. She stepped to the counter. "I know you're thirsty so I fixed you a lemonade." She wrapped her fingers around the cold glass and handed it to him. "What's this about a preacher coming in?"

He upended the glass and guzzled half of the liquid. "Ah, Alma couldn't hold it in."

"She didn't tell me everything."

"I was going to talk to you about it before

the Wenhams arrive. That won't be for a couple of months. We'll be able to move into the other house by then, so I offered for them to take this house. They'll need a place…and we need a preacher and a teacher. There are five children who are old enough to be in school, even Heidi is old enough." He laughed. "She's smart enough, anyway."

"We have is a more immediate problem," Sophy said. "Where are you…our parents going to sleep?"

He finished the drink and set the glass on the counter. She could feel him thinking. Funny how little time it had taken them to read each other's thoughts and feelings. Then he rubbed the back of his neck like he did when considering a problem. "They could take our room, except for the baby." He twisted his mouth. "We'll give them Heidi and Marty's room and set up the children's beds out in the parlor."

That was what she'd been thinking, but she'd wanted him to think of it.

"I better get back to work. We've about got the roof on. That'll leave the siding and windows. By the time the other men have to return to their crops, we'll have the siding on and all that'll be left when Ma and Pa get here is the inside. Pa's really good at carpentry and Ma is a good decorator."

"I'll be more than strong enough to help them."

Sophy

A smile tugged at his lips. "That you will."

She followed him to the porch and he turned to kiss her on the cheek. "Love you."

"Love you back." She hugged her middle and watched him walk away—head high, shoulders straight, everything a man should be.

Somewhere in the back reaches of her mind, she remembered that verse she'd read when she'd been so sure Caleb was leaving to marry another. A promise that God would give her the desire of her heart. Without her realizing it, God had given her the desire of her heart. Caleb.

And she would cherish him all the days of their lives together.

The End

If you enjoyed reading *Sophy*, you'll like all the other books. Each one is a stand-alone story of love and faith. Here is an excerpt from *Betsy* on pre-order now, along with *Rosalee*.

Betsy Excerpt

The man who beckoned to Betsy as she descended the stage steps looked nothing like she'd imagined. He couldn't be her fiancé. Simon Munson described himself as a twenty-five-year-old with black hair and of medium, muscular build. He was thirty-five, if he were a day. He did have black hair. She'd give him that, but his middle was pouchy, nowhere near muscular in her opinion.

Perhaps the chill she felt was due to the weather, and the cold didn't surprise her. It was bound to be colder in Rocky Gap, Montana, than in Bedford Illinois. She pulled her fur lined wood cloak closer and moved toward the man who was smiling a welcome.

It was her fault for not insisting on a photograph, but Mr. Munson's demeanor and personality might make up for a lack of good looks. She wasn't so shallow to judge a book by

Sophy

its cover. Besides, what choice did she have? Her brother, James, had dropped the subtle hints and outright told her she would have to marry or go stay with Aunt Gert, a scurrilous, demanding old lady who expected a destitute niece to be an unpaid servant.

Mr. Munson swept his hat off and bowed as she approached, confirming he was indeed waiting for her. "Miss Holbrook, I presume. You are more lovely than I'd pictured you."

Heat warmed her ears. Truth was, she'd never felt so grimy and unkempt as after the last leg of that train ride. Still, she appreciated his flattery. "Thank you. I'm so glad to finally meet you." She let a nervous laugh slip by. "And finally get off that train."

He chuckled and hooked her by the elbow. "You can freshen up at the ranch house."

"Oh, thank you. I can't wait to see it." Mr. Munson had described the ranch in such specific detail, Betsy already felt like she'd recognize it.

He patted her arm as he took her to a wagon driven by a team of perfectly matched bays. The back of the wagon was filled with crates and gunny sacks—supplies she supposed, but why would he need to buy so much since the ranch house was located only a couple of miles out of the small town of Rocky Gap.

She sneaked a searching glimpse of the town and its few buildings. Not much of a town, but that didn't surprise her. Mr. Munson had warned her that Rocky Gap was much smaller and rustic than Helena, where she'd gotten off the train and rode by stage the rest of the way. Helena was an anomaly, having been built by men who'd become wealthy during the gold rush.

Much of the west was still unsettled. Besides, the Munson ranch covered two thousand acres. There couldn't possibly be much land for others to settle.

Rocky Gap didn't even boast a boarding house or hotel. Nothing much beyond a country store and post office and stage depot. This was why Mr. Munson had explained that they'd have to be wed right away since she'd have to move into the ranch house as soon as she arrived.

He helped her onto the seat and settled a blanket over her before taking up the reins. "The preacher will arrive for supper and he'll marry us then." Mr. Munson smiled at her.

"Do you have a cook?" she asked. Surely as prosperous as he was there would be a cook. She could cook well enough, but not for a group of twenty ranch hands.

"They've all left for the winter," Mr. Munson said. "Sammy's the cook for the crew. I eat with them in the bunkhouse when they're here and do my own cooking in the winter."

She didn't like the sound of that. Was she to be the only woman on the ranch? "You have to

Sophy

do all the work by yourself in the winter?"

"I do what chores I need to. All the cattle has been sold or let out to winter in the canyons. In the spring we have a round up and bring the herds in." He laughed. "Winters can be brutal here. Sometimes I get snowed in for weeks." He reached over to take and squeeze her hand. "Sure will be good to have company this year."

She forced a smile. Somehow she hadn't expected to be so alone, but why she hadn't considered that possibility. But the ranch house was close enough to town to make friends with some of the women, go to church. Maybe they had a sewing circle.

On the edge of town, if one could call it a town, Mr. Munson stopped the wagon. "Stay seated. This won't take but a minute."

He was right, it didn't take but a minute, but in the space of that minute Mr. Munson's mood changed. He offered her no explanation of what had transpired and she didn't want to know, better to let him work out his disappointment in his own mind.

Betsy took advantage of the silence to concentrate on the majestic view of the snow-covered Tetons captured her attention. This was surely beautiful country. It was so different from what she was used to. Stark, but beautiful. She hoped she'd get used to the land.

Mr. Munson must have seen her worried look. He began to tell about ranch life, the

Elaine Manders

routines that meant nothing to her, but she listened politely.

After a while she noticed they'd been traveling a long way. "Shouldn't we be getting to the house soon?"

"It'll take another hour or an hour and a half, I guess."

"I thought the house was only a couple of miles outside of town."

"No, don't know how you got that idea." There was a snarl in his voice that had her slipping as far to the other side of the wagon bench as she could. "No need to keep looking at your watch. My property starts about that close to town, but the house sits in that valley between those two rises ahead. Like you can see, the land is too mountainous and rocky to farm. That's why I raise cattle, but there's no grazing land except in the valley." He said it like any half-brained hound dog would know that.

Though she kept quiet from then on, Mr. Munson broke the silence several times with complaints about the town, his workers, the weather, and especially the burden of keeping up the house without a wife. He left no doubt he wanted a wife for no other reason than to cook, clean, and wait on him.

After another two hours—and she did keep looking at her watch—Mr. Munson drove into the yard of a two-story farmhouse, stopping between the house and the barn.

Sophy

The place was nice and well kept, a house any wife would love to call home, except she'd already decided that wife wouldn't be her. During the wagon ride, Mr. Munson had morphed from a disappointing, but fairly pleasant man to a sullen lout who blamed every difficulty in his life on everyone except himself.

He jumped down. "Take this crate with the food stuffs in the house and get supper on. It'll be dark soon. Your stage was an hour late and that put me way behind with chores."

She had noticed how low the sun had sunk behind the mountains. If she had had time and been in a better mood, she'd have loved to enjoy the sunset that sent out streaks of red, pink, and gold over the snow-covered peaks.

Gaining the ground, she examined the back of the wagon for the crate of food. It was easy to identify with a sack of flour sticking out the top. She couldn't budge the thing and Mr. Munson had already disappeared in the barn, and even if he hadn't, she wouldn't have asked for help. She removed the twenty-five pound sack of flour and found the remaining contents of dried beans, sausage, sugar, and coffee beans manageable.

The inside of the house was in shambles. Pieces of clothing, including underwear, were draped over the furniture. The room held the sour odor, probably caused by glasses and cups of liquid with mold growing in them. The kitchen was worse. Not finding an empty space on the table or counter, she set the first load of food on the floor.

Before leaving to retrieve the flour and beans, she raised the windows. It would take the full day tomorrow to clean this pigsty. Only she wouldn't be here tomorrow. Granny Sraggs always said everyone had a sixth sense—a feeling that something was wrong—and when you got that feeling, you'd better listen to it.

Despite the wonderful marriages Ester and Irene had found through the mail, Betsy's would be a mistake. While she rushed around the kitchen cleaning off a place to work, she sent up prayers of thanks to God for allowing her to see the danger in time. What if she'd married this dangerous man when she'd gotten off the stage?

She glanced out the dingy window to make sure he was still working in the barn.

There was no time to cook beans, but she found a jar of canned peas and a half a haunch of ham. After firing up the stove, she fried slices of ham and made biscuits. That would have to do.

By the time she'd finished washing enough dishes to set the table, she'd made her plans. When the preacher arrived, she'd tell him she'd changed her mind and ask for a ride with him back to town. Surely any Christian man, let alone a preacher, would help and provide a place to stay until morning.

She knew the stage only came through town

Sophy

twice a week, but she'd hire someone to take her to Helena where she'd take the train back home.

The door slammed open, making her jump. Mr. Munson brought in her carpet bag and trunk. He disappeared down the center hallway and returned with a scowl and clenched jaw. She'd have to play along until the preacher arrived.

"Supper is almost ready. When is the preacher coming?" That was the third time she'd asked and he'd yet to answer.

"I smell the coffee. Is that ready?"

"Yes, I'll get you a cup."

He took her by the arm and dragged her into the kitchen. "Go ahead with the coffee. I take it black."

She found a mug on the sideboard where she'd left the washed dishes. After pouring them both a cup, she sat at the other end of the table, a strong desire to put as much distance between them as possible.

He blew on the brew and drank thirstily. She watched his jaw clench as he set the cup down and held her with a squinting gaze. "The preacher isn't coming."

Her heart fell into her stomach and she clenched both hands at her sides. "Why not? If the preacher isn't coming tonight, I'll have to go back to town now." She got to her feet and sped toward the door.

He sprang from his chair and grabbed her by the arm, hauling her back to the table and shoving her into the chair. "You're not going anywhere. The truth is, it's going to be a week or two before we get married."

Fear held her speechless for a moment. "What are you saying? I can't stay here. No decent man would ask that."

"I'm not asking. I'm telling. We can't get married right now because I have a wife and she hasn't died yet. It's not my fault. The doctor said she'd be gone before you got here." He drank the rest of his coffee. "She's hanging on just for spite."

Betsy couldn't believe what he'd just said. "You have a wife and yet advertised for a mail-order bride? Where is your wife?"

"She's at the doctor's. She and his wife were friends, so she'll stay there until she dies, so you don't have to worry about her."

Betsy took a deep breath, praying for calm. Clearly she was dealing with a mad man. "You'll have to sleep in the barn—or I'll have to. Which will it be?" Either way, as soon as daylight, she'd be leaving.

He hunched over the table. "You'll sleep in my bed. As of now, you're my mistress and if you behave, I might make it legal after the old woman dies. Now get that food on the table, I'm hungry."

It was a good thing she didn't have any

Sophy

poison handy as she dished up the ham and biscuits. She didn't know where a bowl was, so she plopped the pot of peas down on the table. He gave her a mean look, but said nothing as he filled his plate. The pulse jumped in his jaw, indicating his rage. She didn't know why he was angry. With his wife for not dying? Was that the doctor's house where he'd stopped on the way? Whoever he'd spoken to, that person had given him unwelcome news.

She took a piece of ham and a biscuit. Knowing she'd need all the energy she could muster if she was to make an escape, she forced the food down her throat. Her brain spun like a locomotive's wheel, grinding out ideas for escape without letting him know.

When he finished eating, he got up. "I'm going to the outhouse. There's a chamber pot for you. You can clean up the kitchen before getting ready for bed."

How gallant of him to give her permission to clean up. Betsy sprang to her feet. Now was her opportunity to escape. If she could make it to the barn before he returned from the outhouse, she'd sneak a horse out and ride bareback to town where she'd ask someone to get the horse back to the Munson ranch, then find someone who'd take her to Helena for pay. She still had enough money to make her way back home sewn inside her skirt.

Granny Scaggs always said you should never go anywhere you couldn't get back from.

Elaine Manders

It was daring, but worth the chance. If she stayed in this house a minute longer, the brute would... She shuddered. He expected her to be his mistress and slave.

She shifted the strap of her carpet bag over her shoulder and opened the front door. Unfortunately, she'd have to leave her trunk, but her brother would come back later and get it. He'd call her all kinds of stupid, and she'd have to agree with him, but he confront Munson. Walt didn't let anyone mess with his family.

As she'd hoped, it was now too dark to see well, making it easy to hide in the shadows. She didn't know exactly where the outhouse was, but usually it was situated at the farthest corner of the back yard.

He must have been hiding in the barn, waiting for her. Munson reached out from the dark and grabbed her by the arm. She screamed.

"Where do you think you're going?"

Anger got the better of her. "I'm leaving and if you try to stop me, my brother will come looking for you and he won't leave enough of you for the vultures."

"That so?" He backhanded her with such force, she fell hard, the blow making her ear ring. She tasted blood on her lip.

Her hair had fallen from its pins and he took ahold of it, dragging her back to the house. She'd underestimated this monster. Only God could save her now. Like any child in trouble, she called out to her Father to save her.

Inside the house, Munson shoved her halfway across the room. "Don't you ever try that again. Now, get into that bedroom and clean yourself up."

Tears and prayers kept flowing as she stumbled to the bedroom. She shut the door behind her. There was a window. The urge to climb out of that window was almost more than she could resist. But how could she block the door. There was no lock, nor a chair to lodge under the handle. A chest of drawers stood on the other side of the room, but it would take more of her strength than she had. Besides, he'd hear her before she got it in place.

Then, when she thought her prayers had failed her, she saw it.

A gun belt hung over the bed's headboard, with a pistol in it. There were bullets on the belt, and she knew how to load a gun. She knew how to shoot too. Papa had taught her. Had taken her hunting with a shotgun. But the pistol was for protection.

With renewed energy, she crossed the room, pulled the pistol out of the holster and broke it open. It was already fully loaded. She squared her shoulders and hid the gun in the folds of her skirt. Her father's words came back to her. "Put space between you and the enemy, don't give him time to react. Fire to kill. A wounded man is worse than a wounded bear.

Her heart beat so fast, she could hardly get a good breath. *Please, Lord, be with me.* She opened the bedroom door and slipped out, then sidled along the wall. The front room had darkened with only the low flames from the fireplace giving light.

Praise God, Munson's back was to her. *Put space between you and the enemy.* As quiet as a mouse trying to get by the barn cat, she moved in backward steps to the door. She slowly turned and lifted the pistol, finding him in its sights.

"I'm leaving."

He swung around and lunged toward her, grabbing for the gun. It fired and he staggered backward.

Horrified, she watched a red circle bloom on the upper left of his white shirt. It was too high to be fatal. *A wounded man is more dangerous than a wounded bear.* She stepped back, pistol raised with hands that shook.

But to her surprise, Munson seemed more stunned than angry. He craned his neck to look at the wound, then his startled gaze met hers. "You shot me, you hussy." Despite the words, his tone was hushed, almost respectful.

"And I'll shoot you again if you try to stop me."

He surprised her again by turning his back to her. "You see any blood back there?" he asked with no more concern than if asking if he had dander on his back.

Sophy

"No."

"I hope you're satisfied. Now I'll have to go see the doc so he can dig the bullet out."

He almost succeeded in making her feel sorry for him. "You can't do that. The journey might cause you to lose too much blood. I'll go tell the doctor to come out here." She still had the gun trained on him. "You'd better go put a cold compress on that wound and lie down or you might bleed out." Hopefully, that would convince him. "I'll get the doctor to bring your horse and pistol back." That ought to tell him she wouldn't be back.

Before he had time to react, she opened stepped out the still open door and fled to the barn. She'd take the few precious seconds to saddle one of the horses, although she could barely see in the dark barn and she wasn't about to light the lantern, even if she knew where it was.

She found the saddle and threw it on Silver Boy's back, then pulled him outside where the light was a little better. After fitting the bridle and cinching the saddle, she hooked her carpet bag on the horn, slipped the gun in her waistband, and mounted the sleepy horse.

Silver Boy was a fine animal, and Betsy couldn't prevent a tinge of envy. She'd never own a horse of this caliber. The ride was fast and smooth, taking less than two hours to reach Rocky Gap.

Elaine Manders

It wasn't hard to find businesses along the main street. Dr. Malcolm Woods had a sign outside his house, clearly one of the best in the town. Doctor's Office and Infirmary. Betsy had to wonder how he kept such a large practice going in this isolated place, although Mr. Munson had told her consumption patients from all over the state came here because the disease was contagious and it was best to keep the patients isolated from the populace. She didn't know why she'd question that. Surely he would know since his wife was here.

The doctor and his sister, who served as his nurse, ran the place. A woman, wearing a white and blue calico dress and a guarded look opened the door. A white apron with an insignia proclaimed her to be the nurse. While Betsy explained the situation, a tall, bearded man came up behind the woman. He was much younger than Betsy had expected, still in his thirties she would guess.

"Where was the wound, Miss Holbrook?" the doctor asked.

Betsy placed her hand high on her left shoulder. "It was here, near the shoulder socket. I don't think it's a life-threatening wound, but the bullet didn't come out, so Mr. Munson sent me to ask you to come tonight."

Another woman had entered the foyer. She laid a hand on Dr. Woods's shoulder. "Must you go out tonight, Malcolm? The air holds ice and snow, and Miss Holbrook says it isn't life

Sophy

threatening."

Betsy presumed this woman, who was strikingly beautiful, must be the doctor's wife.

Dr. Woods patted her hand. "I won't be long, but do stay up for me."

The nurse turned to Betsy. "She's right. The weather promises to turn bad. If you have nowhere else to stay, you're welcome to spend the night here, Miss Holbrook."

Betsy considered the kind offer, but the desire to get as far from Rocky Gap overruled her personal comfort. She would go on with her plan to rent a horse from the livery and arrive in Helena before the morning train pulled out.

"Thank you, but no, I must leave immediately. Doctor, would you please take Mr. Munson's horse with you? Oh, and this." She pulled the pistol from her skirt.

The doctor's dark brows rose, but he took the gun and nodded.

The weather indeed was getting colder. The air held a lot of moisture and a fine, chilly mist descended on Betsy as she walked to the livery stables. The roan gelding provided by the stable boy was an inferior animal to Silver Boy, but the young fellow who looked to be about thirteen, told her the horse was fresh and could make the trip without many rest stops.

By the time she was mounted, tiny ice pellets had her pulling her cloak around her shoulders. She stopped at the necessary by the stage depot and took the time to pull out her other dress from her carpet bag, grateful she'd packed her mittens and matching cap and muffler.

She pulled the dress on over the one she wore, slipped the mittens on under her leather gloves and pulled the knitted cap down over her ears. Finally, she wrapped the muffler around her neck.

The added clothes made movement cumbersome, but held off the cold. She set the gelding in a fast gallop on the road she'd traveled just this morning, only in the opposite direction to Helena.

She'd barely reached the open countryside when the first snowflakes fell. Within minutes a white cloud swirled about her in a wind so fierce she had to hold onto the saddle horn to keep from falling. The snow thickened, making it impossible to see the horse's head.

Dear Lord, help me.

Author's Note

Thank you, dear reader, for reading *Sophy, Book 1, Rescued Widows, Spinsters, and Brides..*

Readers are so important to the success and growth of good Christian fiction. If you enjoyed this book, please help us promote it by letting your friends know through social media and word of mouth. Subscribe to my newsletter and receive a free ebook, *Cloaked in Love*, and announcements about future books.
https://dl.bookfunnel.com/or10xrsvje

Please join my FB group to get updates of upcoming releases and find quizzes and games and fun.
https://www.facebook.com/groups/582237126392288 And, most importantly, pray for me and other authors. The publishing industry is an important way to enlighten the public about the love of God in an entertaining way. Since reviews are more important than ever for books to get noticed, please leave a review at Amazon and Goodreads. I write only for the Lord's glory and the reader's pleasure, so I would much appreciate your opinion.

Books by Elaine Manders

The Annex Mail Order Brides series:
Adela's Prairie Suitor
Ramee's Fugitive Cowboy
Prudie's Mountain Man
The Annex Mail-Order Brides Boxset

Intrigue under Western Skies series:
Book 1, Pursued
Book 2, Surrendered
Book 3, Revealed
Book 4, Escaped

The Wolf Deceivers series:
Book 1, The Chieftain's Choice
Book 2, The Duke's Dilemma
Book 3, The Captain's Challenge

Westward Home and Hearts, a mult-author series:

Book 1, Lacy's Legacy
Book 3, Maggie's Christmas Miracle
Book 5, Bethany's Baby
Book 9, Colleen's Claim
Book 13, Greta's Gift
Book 22, Rachel's Refuge

Brides of Pelican Rapids, a mult-author series:

Book 5, Molly's New Song
Book 10, Hannah's Last Hope
Book 19, Polly's Secret Mission

Georgia Peaches, a multi-author series:

Book 2, A Pursued Heart

Secret Baby Dilemma, a multi-author series:

Book 12, Mail Order Kaitlyn

The Sheriff's Mail Order Bride, a multi-author series:

Book 7, A Bride for Matthew

Also:

The Perfect Gift
The Washwoman's Christmas
Cloaked in Love

About the Author

Elaine Manders writes wholesome, Christian romance about the strong, capable women of history and present day and the men who love them. She lives in Central Georgia with a happy bichon-poodle mix. When not writing, she enjoys reading, sewing, crafts, and spending time with her daughter, grandchildren, and friends. You may contact the author at any of the following.

Facebook:
https://www.facebook.com/elaine.manders.35

Elaine's Friends and Readers Group:
https://www.facebook.com/groups/582237126392288

Email: elainehmanders@gmail.com

Bookbub:
https://www.bookbub.com/authors/elaine-manders

Made in United States
North Haven, CT
08 December 2022